They left the cabin at the same time, and Ez walked with her toward Three as she'd known he would. As safe and well-lit as the area was, it was beyond him to let a woman walk alone in the dark.

"You're right. It's not hard that they need things, but that I might not be able to deliver." He spoke abruptly, his voice strained, the words slow and yet sharp.

The pain evident in his eyes back in the cabin was a palpable presence between them as they walked. She wondered what caused it. What had brought him to this place in the most rural part of Kentucky? Was it an oasis to him as it was to her, or was it a punishment? "None of us can deliver all the time." Her words were as slow as his, but measured. She wanted to offer acknowledgment of his concern, but she didn't feel qualified to give succor to the pain that had no name. At least, not a name she knew.

"No."

His teeth gleamed in an unexpected smile that she knew without being able to see didn't reach his eyes.

"But sometimes the failures are ones you can't get over."

Praise for Liz Flaherty

"A wonderful, wonderful book about life, love, hurt, healing, and finally…redemption."

~ Kyra Jacobs for The Girls of Tonsil Lake

~*~

"…skillfully written and wonderfully told."

~ Cheryl Reavis for The Girls of Tonsil Lake

~*~

"…if you love any kind of romance, you'll love this."

~ LASR for Because of Joe

~*~

"Cleanly written, with wonderful lines that made me sigh and wished I'd written them myself…"

~ Author Mimi Barbour for Because of Joe

~*~

"Liz Flaherty's voice is fresh and fun, entertaining and moving. Her characters come to life and you feel an immediate affinity to them."

~ USA Today Bestselling Author Nan Reinhardt

Life's Too Short for White Walls

by

Liz Flaherty

Life's Too Short for White Walls

COPYRIGHT © 2022 by Liz Flaherty

Cover Art by *Lisa Dawn MacDonald*

The Wild Rose Press, Inc.
PO Box 708
Adams Basin, NY 14410-0708
Visit us at www.thewildrosepress.com

Publishing History
First Edition, 2022
Trade Paperback ISBN 978-1-5092-4156-9
Digital ISBN 978-1-5092-4157-6

Published in the United States of America

Dedication

For the Word Wranglers, past and present. Friends, bloggers, secret-keepers, and people to laugh with every day of the extraordinary journey that is writing books. Thanks for everything, girls!

Acknowledgments

Chapter One

When she couldn't stand the skin-prickling sensation of people feeling sorry for her any longer, Jocelyn Murphy—who'd just spent twenty-five years as Jocelyn Landry—packed all the clothes she hadn't donated to the church thrift shop into two suitcases. Everything else she owned went into a storage unit. She prepaid six months on the space, long enough to find permanence, to find a life in a place away from Dolan Station, Tennessee.

"Are you sure, Joss?" her friend Allie asked for the tenth time. "It's not too late to change your mind. You haven't been back to Banjo Bend since you were a kid, except for funerals and weddings. How can you be sure it's going to be the same?"

"I know it won't." Joss hated how defeated she sounded. "My grandparents and my aunts and uncles are all gone from there. I haven't seen my cousins in years, and I don't even know if the farm is still in the family. I just need to be somewhere different from here, and the farm was a place I was always happy."

She ignored the pity in Allie's eyes, gave her a final hug, and climbed into her SUV. "We split our assets when we got divorced, but Brett was the one who got to keep the life we had. He lives in the house, is still a deacon at church, and sits on the library board. I even check the parking lot for his car when I go to the coffee shop. Every time I see him or Cassie or my mother, it's two steps backward."

"Keep in touch, or I'll have the cops after you." Allie grinned, although the expression failed when she bit her bottom lip. "My husband would have a forgiveness speech for you if he were here. I'm sure he's right, but personally, I'll help you hide the bodies if you can't manage it."

Joss burst into laughter. "He's a pastor. Having his wife be an accomplice in murder wouldn't look good for him." She reached through the open window to grasp her hand. "I'll be fine."

Allie's fingers squeezed hers. "Be safe."

Joss had to bite back a bitter response. Nothing was safe. Not quarter-century marriages to the only person she'd ever dated, kissed, or made love with. Not a job in a place where her ex-husband was on the executive board. Not a sister who'd envied Joss's life so much she moved in and took it, including the husband, the Yorkie, and the house in Dolan Station.

Joss spent her entire life in the Nashville, Tennessee, suburb. She was both happy and fulfilled. Most of the time, she liked being married to Brett Landry. She'd loved being the mother of Sam and Noah, twins who'd grown up so fast she was still amazed by the sheer speed it. She thrived on working at the library three days a week.

That was then, though. Now she and the little blue SUV made their way north and east toward Banjo Bend, Kentucky. The little coal-mining town was her safe place once. She hoped it would be again. The marriage and the job were gone and even Sam and Noah lived clear across the country and didn't need anything from her anymore.

When her mother urged her to forgive Cassie and Brett and support them in their new life together, Joss's last tie to Nashville broke with a snap so sharp it should have been audible. Even the condo she bought as an investment remained just that—she never hung any pictures, brushed color onto the first bland white wall, or unpacked anything beyond her most basic seasonal wardrobe.

Thankful for the car's GPS, she left the highway in eastern Kentucky and meandered through back roads. She and Cassie and their cousins spent long childhood summers here. Their father grew up on a farm tucked into the twisting curves that followed Banjo Creek. As far as Joss knew, family members still lived in the area. The Murphys and her mother were never fond of each other, so the relationship became stilted and slight after Joss's father's death when she was in high school. It disappeared altogether the year her grandmother died, when her mother had insisted the Murphys were "different from us" and Cassie didn't want to visit anymore.

Joss stopped at a café in Banjo Bend—population 946—that promised the best redeye gravy and the most endless cup of coffee in eastern Kentucky. While it wasn't dark yet, the sun had dropped behind the rippling Appalachians a while before, and she wasn't looking forward to driving much farther.

"Is there a motel anywhere close?" she asked the waitress named Romy who brought her food. "Or a B & B?"

The woman, her dark hair in a long ponytail, slid into the other side of the booth. "Let me rest my feet while I think. The only motel in town closes down on Labor Day when the owner hotfoots it to Florida for the winter." She looked over her shoulder, "Hey, Nate, has the campground opened for business yet? I know Ezra McIntire, the guy who bought it, has been working his tail off."

The only other customer in the cafe turned from his seat at the counter. "It has, at least partly. The camp store's open and some of the cabins." He looked at Joss, his expression doubtful. "It's not fancy, though, ma'am. There's electricity and plumbing, but not a lot of much else, I don't think."

"Can you give me directions?" She was tired enough that "not a lot of much else" didn't worry her in the least. "Or just the address. My GPS can get me there."

"Not much to it." Romy got up, going behind the counter and coming back with a glass coffee carafe, refilling Nate's cup as she passed. She sat in the booth again, talking as she poured warmups into Joss's and her own cups. "Just keep driving on this road until you come to the first crossroads outside of town. Hang a right and cross the bridge over the creek. The campground will be about a mile past that—just follow the water. It's on the old Murphy farm, if you're from around here." Romy steepled a finger over her lips. "You look sort of familiar."

Joss looked at her blankly. A campground? The farm was a campground? Belatedly, Romy's comment registered. "I was here sometimes when I was a kid." *Every summer. On the old Murphy farm, swimming and fishing in the creek and camping in the woods with Marley, Grayson, June, and Seven. Funny Seven, who got his name because someone left the "t" out of Steven, and no one ever bothered correcting it.*

Cassie went, too, but always reluctantly…at least until they got there, spilling out of the family car and running to meet Gran on the path in front of the farmhouse.

She'd smelled like bread and the garden and love, and in Joss's memory, she'd been able to get her arms around all of them at once. Knowing the land was no longer in the family hurt more than Joss would have expected. She added it to the list of losses that had already rained down in the past year and had to swallow panic. When would it stop?

On the way to the farm, she reminded herself to be grateful for all that was good, a Sunday school lesson that had carried her through worse days than these. Well, maybe not worse, but other bad ones. "The boys are all right. I have enough money to last a while if I'm careful. Watching the sun go down in the Appalachians is always a gift. That redeye gravy was the best I've ever eaten, and Romy filled my commuter cup at no charge. Not a bad list."

The sign at the end of the narrow road back to the farm invited her to *Banjo Creek Cabins and Campground*, and she turned in, stopping for a moment to look at her surroundings. Every kind of deciduous tree that made its home in Kentucky canopied the graveled driveway. Leaves were just beginning to change color, and a few of them had drifted to the ground. The grass that grew on either side of the lane was tall and unkempt.

Joss frowned. Her grandfather would have been out there with the farm tractor and its pull-behind mower taking care of the overgrowth. Or one of the grandkids would—they'd all loved driving the squat little tractor.

Halfway between the road and the house—at least, where the house used to be—she stopped again so a few whitetail deer could saunter across in front of her. They stopped to favor her with an unblinking stare, and she grinned back.

Her grandparents' farmhouse was indeed where it had always been, nestled into the woods with the red, gambrel-roofed barn standing sentinel behind it. The building looked neglected. No, not neglected, but lonely…as if no one cared about it. During the summers here, cats and a dog always sprawled on the porch, as well as on the slatted wooden swing and a pair of rocking chairs. Gran's lace curtains had hung at the windows. She'd changed the colors of the shutters and trim every few years, painting the floorboards of the porch to match. They were black now, although chipped and faded. No wonder the house looked lonely—it looked sad, too.

A small building sat by the road. It appeared to be the office and the camp store, and, like Gran's shutters, it needed painting in the worst way.

With a sigh, Joss parked and climbed out of the car, hitching her purse over her shoulder. The accommodations didn't look promising, but they were the only ones she could reach before dark, and she was too tired to go any farther.

The sound of country music drifted into the cluttered and seemingly uninhabited office. An almost-empty liquor bottle sat on the desk behind the counter, along with a computer and a printout of a crossword puzzle, half completed. The puzzle was a hard one, and it took all she had not to go and see what she could do with it. She hadn't brought a printer, so until she settled in somewhere, her puzzling would be confined to the book of *The New York Times* puzzles Allie gave her.

So worn she was tempted to touch it in search of softness, a flannel shirt hung over the back of the desk chair. A door left ajar showed shelves of linens and cleaning supplies.

No one was around, though, and she didn't see a way to summon anyone. She looked into the adjoining room at what was indeed the camp store and didn't see anyone there, either. A red, plastic coffee container containing some bills and coins sat beside the cash register. A note printed in bold Times New Roman offered, *Honor system. Pay here or come by and pay in the morning.*

Darkness filtered into the rooms as she stood there, and she couldn't see a light switch anywhere. The only illumination came from the computer screen, which had a picture of a military helicopter.

The rack of tourist pamphlets and maps was a mess. It looked as if it had been rearranged by a three-year-old—one like Noah, who even at twenty-four left chaos in his wake wherever he went. Joss set about picking the pamphlets up from the floor and pulling them out of their haphazard arrangement in the slots. She stacked them in neat little piles on the counter.

The sudden appearance of light overhead startled her. A full handful of flyers shot into the air and cascaded down over her head and shoulders. When a gruff male voice spoke, she dropped the rest of them.

"You thinking of going to all those places?"

****

7

Ezra McIntire set his tool pouch in one of the chairs on the office porch and stepped inside, reaching overhead to pull the chain on the fixture that provided light to the cluttered room. He really did need to clean it up some.

He didn't mean to scare her.

Ez rested his gaze on a woman with red hair, wearing a Vanderbilt University sweatshirt, slim jeans, and a cluster of tourist pamphlets that hadn't hit the floor yet. He'd have to pick them up again. He'd done that once today already, when the little kids from Cabin Four managed to empty the whole display rack without their parents saying a single word.

Whoever the redhead was, she was pretty. She looked…nice. Also ridiculous with flyers falling all over and around her. Who was she? There weren't any reservations beyond the ones who'd checked in that afternoon, and Banjo Creek wasn't a place people happened onto accidentally. Her eyes, a clear, almost crystalline blue, widened at his question.

"Not all of them at once," she said, "and not after dark."

It took him a second to realize she was answering his question, and her answer sounded like she wanted to stay. Unless she had a tent in the back of that SUV out there, she'd likely want a cabin, too. None of them were ready—at least, not ready enough for someone who looked like her. Cabin Three was clean, but the linens weren't there yet. Margaret, who'd come with the campground, sometimes forgot to check the cabin refrigerators for leftovers or containers of bait.

"Is there something I can do for you?" Even to himself, he sounded both sullen and impatient, as if it were her fault he was in a perpetual bad mood.

"Do you have a vacant cabin, Mr….?" She raised an eyebrow.

Supercilious. It was a favorite crossword clue, and she'd nailed it with that eyebrow. "McIntire. Just Ez. Not one that's entirely ready, no. Depending on which way you're heading, I'd advise you to drive on over toward Prestonsburg. It's less than an hour away, and there are a couple of motels between here and there."

"Can you describe 'not entirely ready' for me?" Patience weighted her voice. "Because I'm 'not entirely ready' to get back on the road. I haven't driven through these hills in more years than I can remember, and I don't want to do it after dark. I'll pay whatever you say." Her shoulders slumped. "I just need to stop."

He wanted a bourbon and soda and a bologna sandwich. Maybe to work the rest of today's puzzle or to read a couple of chapters of one of the books on the pile beside his chair at home. The day had been long enough already, but he thought hers had probably been longer. Even her hair seemed to have grown limp since he'd walked inside, and that was saying something about curls as springy as hers were.

"Cabin Three." He sounded resigned and less than welcoming, even to himself. "It's a family cabin, with two bedrooms, which I'm sure you don't need, but it's clean. I'll just charge the single cabin rate. Let me get the linens." He nodded at the screen and keyboard on the counter. "The page is ready to go there. If you know how to use one of those things, go ahead and enter your information." He went into the supply room without waiting to see if she complied. A moment later, as he searched out towels and sheets, he heard the computer's keys tapping. He stacked a little bunch of complimentary items on top of the linens, wondering if she'd eaten. Not that Banjo Bend offered that many choices, especially after the sidewalks rolled up at dusk, but he wondered anyway. He went back into the office.

"This is where my mail is going," she said, "but I don't have an address right now."

He looked at the information she'd entered. "Murphy, huh? That's a common name around here. You related?"

"This was my grandparents' farm when I was a kid."

She must be related to Gray, whose mother had grown up on this farm, or maybe she was married to someone who was. Either way, it was her business, not his. "Do you want anything from the camp store, Ms. Murphy?"

She didn't answer for a moment. "No. Thank you. Sorry. I haven't been a Murphy for twenty-five years, and it still surprises me when someone calls me that. Just Joss will be fine."

No wonder she was new at traveling alone; she had the look of being freshly divorced, something he should have recognized. Nearly everyone he knew had worn it at one time or another. Not him, but almost everyone else. "There's coffee in the cabin, and the café in town opens early. The bakery delivers donuts here every morning, too." A little restaurant building stood on the campground, too, but it wasn't open yet. Ez wasn't sure it ever would be.

He wasn't sure about much at all.

Being a country boy ended when Ezra McIntire enlisted at seventeen, thirty-one years ago. He lived either in base housing or in apartments off-base during his entire military career. When he retired, it was with no urge to resume milking cows, planting crops, or any of the other things he'd been so eager to leave that morning he got on the bus to Great Lakes.

Ez liked things like city utilities, trash and recycle pick-up, and grocery stores and restaurants within a mile or so's radius. He liked small, neat yards—preferably seeded and mowed by someone else. He preferred the airport to be twenty minutes away, entertainment venues close enough to go to without spending the night somewhere, and a variety of restaurants to choose from. The band he'd played with in the navy had called themselves Inside City Limits because they'd all been determined to make being urban their lifestyle.

Well, four of the five of them, anyway. Grayson Douglas, who had the physique of a basketball player and the soul of a poet, had wanted nothing more than to return to the place in the middle of the hills and woods of eastern Kentucky where he'd grown up. Instead, he became a diplomat who made his home in any number of foreign countries.

When the campground that had once been the Murphy farm went up for auction after being abandoned, Gray called Ez. "You'll find the peace you need there. If you don't buy it, I will—no problem there—but I think it would be a good place for you. When you don't need it anymore, I'll buy it then, too."

Because his trust in the former drummer of Inside City Limits was absolute, Ez bought the property unseen and hauled his PTSD-burdened self four hours through the mountains from Virginia to Kentucky to live. Six months later, he was fairly sure he'd made a mistake. But the redhead with tired eyes didn't care if he had or not—she just wanted a place to stay.

He stepped outside the office with her and pointed toward the two rows of cabins, many of them partially hidden by the trees. "The second one on that side. You can follow me over."

"All right."

He drove the campground's utility task vehicle toward the cabin, wondering if she felt uncomfortable here in this isolated place where, as far as he knew, the only person she'd seen was a scruffy-looking has-been navy pilot.

She parked beside him at the cabin and got out of her car. "That was our tree." She pointed at the big sycamore that offered privacy from the inhabitants of Cabin Two. "We had a treehouse in it. We used to sleep there in the summer when it was so hot we couldn't stand the house and Gran and Gramps couldn't stand us anymore."

He thought tears streaked her cheeks, but he wasn't sure and didn't want to draw attention to them if there were. He'd already scared her out of her wits—he didn't want to go digging into what might be making her unhappy. "We did that when we were kids, my brother and me." He hadn't thought of that in years. He wondered how Silas was. He missed him.

At least the cabin smelled fresh. Margaret always opened all the windows when she cleaned. "God's good, clean air's better than all the spray stuff you can use," she said with a deprecatory snort when he suggested she try it.

"This is nice." Joss sounded surprised.

He couldn't blame her. The entire campground needed work.

"I didn't expect a kitchenette."

"They don't all have them. The ones on the other side have two units, with just a bedroom and bath in each one. Fishermen and honeymooners aren't usually interested in kitchens."

She chuckled, the sound deep and musical. "I'm sure you're right." She offered her hand. "Thank you for letting me have the cabin. I really didn't want to sleep in my car in your driveway, and I'm afraid that was my next best option."

"Let me make the bed." He liked her hand and didn't particularly let it go, but making the bed made a lot more sense. "We're not so into roughing it that we expect you to do that."

"I'll help you."

He wasn't going to argue. He didn't like any of the housekeeping facets of the job, although he could still bounce a quarter off any bed he made. She probably could, too, he was surprised to notice. "Were you in the military?"

"No, but I was married for a long time. It's good training."

Her voice was dry, as if he'd opened up something painful. He supposed that was common enough—his mother had always wanted to fix his father, too, and the harder she tried, the more the old man pushed back. "Yeah." Ez folded the blankets back. "Marriage needs to be good for something." He was a fan of training, after all, but he didn't think getting married was a worthwhile way of getting it.

He didn't say anything else, and she didn't either.

He showed her what channels were on the TV—not all that many—and told her a few books were in the office she could borrow if she wanted. "Rest well." He opened the door.

"Do you live in the house?"

He frowned. "The house?"

"The farmhouse."

"Oh, sorry. No. The person who originally made the farm into a campground built a log house on the creek. I live in it. The farmhouse is empty, on the long list of things that need doing."

"Would it be okay if I went inside it?"

"Sure. Stop by the office tomorrow, and I'll give you the key." He nodded briefly. "Goodnight, Ms. Murphy. Joss."

She smiled.

The expression was so fleeting he wasn't sure he'd really seen it, although an adolescent fluttering behind his ribs assured him he had.

"Goodnight, Mr. McIntire. Ez."

Chapter Two

Joss hadn't walked for pleasure or exercise since she pushed the twins through the subdivision in their double stroller the summer she and Allie decided they'd lose their baby weight by speed-walking the neighborhood. That being the case, she surprised herself the next morning when she put on a jacket and carried her coffee around the campground. The sky lent bright and blue promise to the day. Campers sat at picnic tables outside their RVs or tents, waving as she walked past. She felt the sting of unwanted aloneness, but not too much. The "not too much" was progress—at least, that was how she was going to look at it.

Learning the hundred and sixty acres she and her cousins had run all over when they were kids was no longer a working farm had been a jolt, but the property had been put to good use. Wooded areas remained, although roomy campsites lined the old logging road that curved through the trees. Tent sites filled one area, with larger RV spots claiming another. The banks of the creek had been cleared. The swimming area was clearly demarcated, and sand had been brought in to create a beach.

The picnic pavilion her grandfather had built on the foundation of the old tobacco barn was still there, much improved, with stone fireplaces at each end and restrooms nearby. Horseshoe pits, a basketball court, tennis courts, and a playground were all within easy walking distance with paved paths.

She thought about walking farther down the creek toward the barely-there village of Colby's Hollow, but her cup was empty and her stomach rumbled a reminder that she hadn't eaten since the night before. The sensation was both odd and pleasing. Most of the hollowness she'd felt over the past couple of years had been born from distress and despair.

In retrospect, she didn't know why she'd thought she was special, that her marriage was going to last forever when so many others didn't. She and Brett survived things that wrecked the unions of friends. His infidelity early on, the miscarriage of a child so wanted that even twenty years later thinking of the loss could bring Joss to tears, the realization that their values were more different than they were alike.

Even after the final betrayal, she somehow expected him to be fair. She thought he'd respect her contributions to their life together. But Brett was a very astute banker. By the time the assets had been divided, they were somewhat diminished. He truly had won most of the bread, and it ended up in his breadbox. He had to give her half the value of the house, though, and he hadn't asked for half of her retirement account, so she was better off than she might have been. Better off than some of her friends.

She pushed away thoughts of her ex-husband and her sister—something that was becoming increasingly easy to do, another odd and pleasing sensation. It was okay, Allie had said, to be angry and hurt and vengeful, but if it took over her life "they've won."

Not letting them win had become a daily mantra,

one Joss repeated until she started to believe it. She did, it was true, still mourn the life she'd lived and loved, but she was finding she missed the kitchen in her house more than she did Brett.

At the camp store, she bought a half dozen eggs—brown ones, the kind her grandmother's chickens had laid—a half pound of bacon, and a half loaf of bread. She almost never ate breakfast, but the hunger had become a real thing.

Ezra McIntire, busy checking people in and answering questions, handed her the key to the farmhouse without comment.

She smiled her thanks and left the office, stopping to straighten the pamphlets again. She prepared her breakfast and sat on the cabin's little front porch to eat it. After washing the dishes and making her bed, she went out again, walking purposefully toward the farmhouse. The closer she got, the faster she walked.

What a happy place it had been. Farm visits were the only times she wasn't "the other one" to everyone except her father. Her grandparents referred to all the cousins as the Banjo Strings, which annoyed Joss's mother. However, most things that had to do with the Murphys annoyed her mother. In all fairness, the irritation worked both ways.

The slatted wooden swing on the porch, like virtually everything else, needed painting. But the key turned smoothly in the lock, and Joss pushed the door open, stepping onto the wide pine boards that floored the entire house. The floor was dusty—Joss could practically hear Gran tsking.

The memories were a sensory assault. She could almost smell her grandmother's apple pie, autumn's first fires in the living room fireplace, and the forever scent of yeast. Gran had baked bread on a nearly daily basis because, as she told her granddaughters, it was cheaper than therapy and kept her from killing Granddad all the years they were married.

The painted cupboards in the big old kitchen remained, but all the appliances were gone. A gap in the cabinetry indicated someone had installed a dishwasher at some point—the plumbing was still there. The big soapstone sink remained under the window that faced the woods.

Other than dust, the house was clean, and some furnishings still there, as if her grandmother had left it the day before instead of years ago. A fire was laid neatly in the fireplace, and all the walls had been painted off-white. Joss chuckled and shuddered at the same time as she went up the creaky back stairs to the second story. Gran would have hated the white walls as much as she did.

The upstairs hadn't changed at all. The farthest back bedroom, the smallest one, was still painted the peculiar but attractive shade of teal that happened when you mixed all the colors from the other rooms to have enough paint to finish the last one. The white metal frame of the bed she'd slept in leaned against the wall.

The cousins' progressive heights, with their names included, were still inscribed on the doorjamb of the upstairs bathroom. Gray had been six foot three at last measure—Joss wondered if he'd stopped growing yet. She hadn't seen him in more years than she could remember. She'd been the shortest, although Marley had been barely an inch taller.

Marley. Just thinking about her made Joss's heart

ache. She wondered how she was, if she was happy in the group home where she lived.

She went down the front stairs and sat in the rocking chair near the fireplace, her grandmother's chair. Her grandfather's recliner was gone. He used to fall asleep in it, never minding when grandchildren crawled all over him.

With the sharpness of new grief, Joss remembered his chair was the only place she could sleep the desolate summer her father died. Her grandparents had left her to it, covering her with a quilt, brushing her hair back from her face, and kissing her cheek that stayed chapped by the tears that never seemed to stop.

She didn't realize until she miscarried her baby how great their own grief must have been. They'd lost their son. Sitting in Gran's chair, she wept again—for her father, her grandparents, the baby she'd wanted and lost, and for the life she'd given up. She cried for golden-haired Cassie and the relationship they'd probably never have again. Lastly, she wept for the little girl Joss had been, with her carroty hair and freckles and awkwardness that no amount of her mother's exasperation had helped.

At some level of consciousness, she must have heard the door open, because she wasn't frightened when a voice spoke.

"I've thought about renting it out for family reunion groups or other gatherings. It could probably sleep at least a dozen comfortably. And then I considered making it a B & B. Of course, I usually think about that after several shots of bourbon. What do you think?"

His voice was low and slow and gravelly and as

comfortable to hear as the water in the creek had been the night before. She could easily lean up against the faded plaid of his flannel shirt and wail about her world gone wrong. The very thought made her stiffen and straighten in the chair. She searched in her pocket for a tissue, remembering abstractedly that Gran had always carried a soft cotton hankie that smelled of sunshine and homemade soap.

Her pocket yielded a paper napkin, and she blew her nose on its roughness and wiped the back of her hand over her eyes. "Sorry," she said. "Nostalgia time." She drew a long breath, then another, willing herself to stop shuddering with leftover tears. "This was always my safe place. It wasn't a popular term then, but that's what it was. I think it would be nice for family reunions or just retreats. Gran would like that. I can't really picture it as a B & B."

He stepped farther into the room and pulled another chair over to set it on the other side of the fireplace.

She wasn't sure the old, armless rocker would hold his weight. She held up a warning hand, then let it drop when the chair accepted him without complaint.

"I like that it's a safe place," he said. "Tell me about her, about your gran."

It took a minute to gain enough composure to talk about Esther Murphy. Ez didn't seem to mind waiting. Joss looked around. "She'd hate all this white. She said the only place for white walls was on a fifty-seven Chevy."

"That explains the colors upstairs and in the kitchen?"

"She'd buy all the mixed colors that never got

picked up at the hardware store in town." Joss laughed, relishing the memory. "They used to be all over the downstairs, too. Granddad walked into the bathroom one day when he came in from the fields, turned around, and walked right out again. He said he was danged if he was going to live with a room the color of baby poop."

After a minute of surprisingly comfortable silence, he spoke. "Forgive me, but you don't look like Banjo Creek. You look more like seven-figure-income suburbia. I'm curious. Why are you here?" As soon as the words were out of his mouth, he shook his head. "I'm sorry—not my business." He started to get up. "I'll leave you alone."

"No, don't go." Another surprise—she hadn't expected to say that. "I don't mind. I'm here because I couldn't stand being where I came from anymore, and this farm was the only place I could think of to go. I haven't been here in…I can't even think how many years, and I should have called first. Or at least tried to check with my cousins."

"It was probably a shock, seeing not only that a campground had replaced hayfields, but that said campground is on the seedy side."

It had been, but the good night's sleep and the morning's walk had given Joss perspective. "My dad always called it a hardscrabble farm. The only reason it made money at all was because of the tobacco crop, and Gran hated tobacco even more than she hated liquor." She chuckled, pushing with her feet to set the rocker in motion. "Actually, she only pretended to hate liquor, because she thought it would keep us kids from drinking. She made rhubarb wine that was to die for.

Everyone had it at their weddings." She softened with the memories. "She and Granddad danced at all of them."

"Didn't the logging make money?"

"It probably did. I was little enough not to know, but I think Gran mourned every tree that went down. As soon as the woods were thinned enough to help their growth, Granddad stopped the logging. He always kept the road up, though." They'd ridden bicycles on it, going through the woods to the creek to swim even when a more direct path was faster.

"I'm glad he did. It was perfect for the campground. Other than laying fresh gravel, it was one thing that didn't have to be changed."

She smiled at him. "What about you, Ezra McIntire? Why are you here? Retired military?"

"Got it in one."

The tone of his voice told her there was more to the story than that.

"A friend—I think you're probably related to Grayson Douglas—told me about this campground, and here I am." From the front pocket of his flannel shirt, his phone chimed. He took it out and squinted at the screen.

"Gray's my cousin. He's a sweetheart."

He grinned and shook his head. "None of us ever referred to him quite that way." He got to his feet. "Duty calls. And stopped-up toilets. Something Gray didn't warn me about."

He left a sensation of emptiness behind him, something that made her laugh at herself. It also put some heat in her cheeks, and she had no intention of examining the reason.

She made notes on her phone as she walked through again, mentally making one bathroom into two and adding another to the back bedroom, using the dormer at the top of the stairs. The addition would cut down on the natural light that streamed through the hall, but it would make three en suites on the second floor. Another one was downstairs that her grandparents had built on when they no longer wanted to climb the stairs. A half-bath connected with the laundry and mudroom off the back porch. The attic could be made into…something, and the house had a dry walk-out basement, but making them into living space would take a lot of money. She didn't know where Ez stood on the financial angle, but she was sure the house would make a great vacation rental. He'd earn his investment back in plenty of time to make it worthwhile.

She continued the tour of the campground, making notes she hoped she'd be able to make sense of later. The small restaurant was in a clearing near the road. She stood in the middle of the parking area and looked around, mystified by the building's location. Closer examination showed her it had been built recently, although its design closely matched the large barn beside the house. A wooden quilt square hung in the rounded peak, and a broad porch invited rocking and playing checkers.

She didn't want bacon and eggs again, no matter how hungry she was when she finished exploring. If she was staying a few days, she was going to have to buy some food or else visit Romy at the café a few times. More of that gravy would taste good.

No cars sat at the office, so she went that way to give Ez back the key to the house.

A new notice hung on the bulletin board inside the door. *Help Wanted* was printed in large black letters. She stopped to read the job description underneath. "Do you have trouble keeping help?"

"We do, and it's hard to imagine why." Ez spoke from behind the counter. "Housekeeping part time. Painter part time. Mowing and/or snow removal part time. Tasks as the job demands. Hours vary. Pay sucks. No benefits." A ghost of a smile crossed his face. "As you can imagine, people are beating down the door to fill the position."

"I'm going into Banjo Bend for lunch. Do you want me to hang a sign at the café?"

"You don't have to."

"I didn't think I did. Is there anywhere else you'd like me to put one?"

"The library has a pretty popular bulletin board in the vestibule in front."

She remembered the library. It sat on a downtown lot surrounded by wrought iron fence. A statue of a woman on a horse stood in the flower garden in front, seeming to welcome visitors. The town had been served for years by a "pack horse librarian." Not until the 1960s did the city buy the big, brick Victorian once owned by someone who'd been something disgraceful during the Civil War and turn it into a library. She hoped it hadn't been replaced by a new and improved model. "Is it still in the Tolliver house? I loved that place." Gran used to let the cousins go to the bridge that crossed the creek at its narrowest point and walk into town. They'd go to the library, the park, and the Big Dipper ice cream stand.

He tapped a few keys on the computer to print two

more signs, extending them toward her. "I don't know. It's across Wallace Street from the little park in the center of town."

"That's it. Is the little bridge still down at Colby's Hollow where you can walk across and shortcut it into Banjo Bend?"

His expression showed confusion. "I don't know. I haven't been to Colby's Hollow."

She pointed. "It's that way. Just follow the creek through the woods. When I was a kid, there were four houses, a tavern where Granddad said it wasn't safe to go after dark, and a church."

"Oh, I've been there. I didn't know it had a name. The bridge is still there, just for bicycles and people on foot. It's part of the trail system. It's a nice walk or bike ride."

"Do you have bikes for rent?"

"Not yet."

He had a lot of "not yet" going on. She hoped he was successful with all his ideas. At least, the ones that would be good for the property and that her grandparents wouldn't refer to as "downright foolish" if they were here to observe. "Do you need anything from town?" If he was shorthanded, it might be difficult to get away. Offering help seemed like the polite thing to do.

"Not today," he said, "but thank you for asking. If you go tomorrow, I might send a list, if you wouldn't mind. I'll pay you for the trouble."

"No trouble." And it wasn't, although, politeness aside, it seemed like an odd request. Banjo Bend was probably less than two miles away. She'd have thought he'd drive there every day for one thing or another.

However, she'd never run a business, either.

When she reached the café, noticing for the first time the sign that referred to it as *Romy's Place*, the lunch crowd—assuming there had been one—had dissipated. A couple of the window booths were occupied, but she was able to slide into a vacant one.

"Coffee?" From behind the counter, Romy lifted a cup in invitation.

"Please."

"The special's chicken and dumplings with mashed potatoes and steamed broccoli on the side to unclog your blood vessels after eating all those carbs. Or you can have anything on the menu except the grilled chicken breast—the whole town's on a health kick, and I ran out." The waitress and apparent namesake for the cafe, who was closer to Joss's own age than she'd originally thought, set down a full cup and a miniature cream pitcher.

"I'll have the special." Joss hadn't had chicken and dumplings for far too long. The food was in front of her in minutes, steaming and inviting.

Romy refilled coffee for one table, accepted payment from the occupants of the other, and came to Joss's booth carrying a cup and an insulated carafe. "Do you mind if I join you?"

"Please do." Joss gave the woman her full attention. She did look familiar, more so than she had the day before, but she couldn't place her. "Is this your restaurant?"

"Mine and the Banjo Bend branch of Eastern Kentucky First Bank." Romy got to the point. "You said you came here as a kid. Did we know each other then?"

"I'm Joss, one of the Murphy grandkids."

"Oh, I should have figured it out. Cassie and I were the same age, although we didn't really get along. It's nice to see you." Romy extended a hand across the table. "I was Roma Sue Myers in those days. No one dared call me Romy back then—my mother was convinced nicknames were works of the devil."

Joss remembered then. Cassie had resented that some of the boys liked tomboy Roma Sue better than her. "Aren't you and Millie sisters?"

"Cousins. Millie spent summers with us, though. She lived the rest of the year in Louisville. Still does, come to that. She's an attorney there."

"She and my cousin Gray were married." Joss had missed their wedding. She'd been far too pregnant to even consider a trip to Louisville—at least, that's what her mother and Brett insisted, and she went along. She always went along.

"For about fifteen minutes, as I remember it."

"I think you're right." She didn't know what had happened, only that Gray had been sad for a long time. "How is Millie?"

"Okay. She comes down every now and then." Romy's hazel eyes met hers, then dropped. "Where is Seven?"

Joss sighed. "I don't know. The rest of us at least send Christmas cards and go to each other's weddings, but it's as if Seven fell off the edge of the earth."

They talked while she ate her lunch and Romy drank her coffee. Then they continued talking over pieces of lemon meringue pie and more coffee.

The group home where Marley lived had once been a boarding house. The big old house where Grayson had lived with his parents was now a mortuary. June and Marley's parents' "company house" had been razed when the nearby coal mine closed. A store promising nothing inside cost more than a dollar was now on the site. The trailer court down near the creek where Seven had lived with his mother had become a nice little retirement village in recent years.

"The town's actually improved since the coal mine closed," said Romy, "although there's still a ton of poverty. Some of the mine towns just rolled up their sidewalks and died. Banjo Bend didn't do that."

Joss was glad. She loved the atmosphere of the little town. She had to backtrack to leave Ez's poster at Romy's when she left. "I forgot." She handed it to the restaurant proprietor.

"I hope he gets some good help from this." Romy shook her head, thumb-tacking the sign up in an obvious place. "He works hard, and I think he's nice, but he stays to himself. He never even comes to town unless he has to. There's a story there, but I don't know what it is and wouldn't say if I did. Nice as Banjo Bend is, it's as bad about gossip as anyplace, and I don't want to be part of the wrong things being said."

"That's nice to hear. I agree with you that there's a story, but I guess it's his to tell. Or not."

"Right." Romy stepped back. "There we go. The Banjo Bend Employment Office at your service. Do you have one of these for the library? The bulletin board there is like the town crier for everyone who's not on social media."

"I do."

"The board's just inside the door—you can't miss it—and there's a box of push pins right there on the table."

"Shouldn't I ask someone?"

Romy looked thoughtful. "Wouldn't hurt. As far as the town's concerned, you are a stranger, after all. At least until they all know you're a Murphy."

Although her boys were still Landrys and she loved them more than her life, Joss felt pretty happy right this minute about being a Murphy again. She walked through the park to the library, enjoying the warmth of the air and grateful that for today at least, it wasn't humid. Romy was right—the town had certainly not given in to the losses created by the mine's closing. Although the changes from when she'd been here last were obvious, the town still felt the same, offering that atmosphere she'd thought about earlier.

The modifications in Banjo Bend's small library were the same as the ones that had taken place in the suburban one where Joss had worked. More movies and audiobooks filled the shelves than actual paper-and-ink volumes. The card catalogs had disappeared, but the curved oak desk remained in the same place as it had been a generation ago.

The young woman behind it looked up with a smile.

Joss asked if she could hang the poster on the bulletin board.

She nodded. "There should be room on it—I cleared off everything this morning that should have been gone a week ago." She laughed.

Joss laughed with her. "I'm just out at the campground for a few days," she said. "Thank you for your help."

"Of course." The librarian extended her hand. "I'm

Cady Whittier. Enjoy your stay."

Driving back to the campground with a few groceries in the backseat of her car, Joss celebrated the fact Banjo Bend was home in a way she desperately needed. On her next trip to town, she would find Marley and take her to lunch. She wondered if her cousin still liked hot dogs and mashed potatoes with potato chips on the side. The combination had horrified Gran, but she'd prepared it anyway—giving the rest of the cousins the stink-eye if they so much as looked askance at Marley's beloved Minnie Mouse plate.

Joss stopped under the canopy of trees that led back to the campground, opening her car window so she could breathe in the scent of early September. For a person as busy as she'd always been to stare the future in the face with no idea what she was going to do with it was hard. She would give herself time to decide, time to take more deep breaths and get over the feeling of dread that seemed to accompany her everywhere. Although she didn't have enough money to last forever, it would carry her for a while.

She gazed up at the trees, noting the colors of the leaves were already changing and that the air smelled different—not just the day's lack of humidity. Rather, she supposed, the scent was of things dying, but she wasn't going to think of it that way. To her, it was going to be all about starting over. Starting new in this beloved place that still felt like home.

Chapter Three

Well into the afternoon, the occupant of Cabin Three was still gone. Ez had changed lightbulbs, run the leaf-blower, and set up the PA system for open mic night in the pavilion while Margaret ran the office and the camp store. He wondered occasionally where Joss had gone—Banjo Bend didn't have enough going on to keep her there all afternoon. If she hadn't left her things behind, he'd think she was gone for good. The idea disturbed him much more than was called for, and the sound test he did for the microphones sounded even grumpier than usual.

Back at the office, Margaret took one look at him and told him he was going to scare off potential customers if he went around wearing that look on his face.

He grinned to please her and didn't mind when the silver-haired woman gave him a smacking kiss on his unshaven right cheek. "You knew the people who owned this place when it was a farm, didn't you?" He poured a can of soda over ice and added a couple of fingers of bourbon.

"Sure, I did. Their daughter Dorie was my best friend until she passed away. I went steady with one of the boys until he went into the army. Michael." She smiled, although sadness touched her eyes. "He met someone else while he was in training. I married

31

Danny, and we moved to Prestonsburg." Margaret straightened things on the counter, none of which needed it. "Michael died a long time back. I hope he was happy."

"You didn't know the next generation then, the cousins?"

"I know Marley, of course, and I've met her sister June—she's the one who's a nun. Not the others, though."

"Joss is one of them, the lady in Cabin Three." He regretted the disclosure as soon as the words were out of his mouth. He didn't talk about campers by name. Many of them came to Banjo Creek for private reasons, and that privacy needed to be safe with him. He didn't think that was the situation with Joss, but talking about her wasn't his business nevertheless.

Margaret nodded, her soft bob swishing past her cheeks. "I'm done for the day if you're okay here," she said. "Anyone coming in for the evening hours?"

"Jed is as soon as he gets out of class." He named the most dependable of the part-time help. Jed Carver was studying to be a park ranger, and he loved the hours spent at the campground; there just weren't enough of them for either the student or Ez. "You coming back to listen to music tonight? I've seen you watching Wil DeWitt out of the corner of your eye."

Margaret winked at him. "I think he might be watching me back, too." She blew him a kiss and left.

Ez waved her off, grateful for the hundredth time that she'd come with the campground when he bought it. He was restocking the water and soda cooler in the store when he heard the office door open. "I'll be right out." He filled the last shelf, closed the door, and stepped into the other room. His heart gave an irritating leap when he saw the redhead standing at the counter. "Joss. You need something?"

"Romy said there was music here tonight. Is that right?"

"Yeah. Open mic. Lots of guitar players and singers. Some mountain dulcimers, mandolins, and banjos, too. It's at the pavilion at seven."

"Do we bring things? Refreshments?"

He raised an eyebrow, considering. "No, although the soda and water machines are in there. Refreshments or even concessions would probably be welcome."

She nodded. At the door of her car, she turned back. "I'd like to stay a while. At least a week. Is the cabin available for that long?"

"It's open until Thanksgiving weekend. The place fills up then for a camping association festival that opens the holiday season." He had a lot to get done before then. He certainly hoped the posters produced some viable candidates.

Meanwhile, he wasn't at all unhappy she was staying for a week—or more. He watched her walk to her car. A bounce that hadn't been there before lightened her step, and he wondered who she'd seen in Banjo Bend that had given it to her. She waved at Jed when he dashed past her, and Ez chuckled when the kid did a double take before waving back.

"Sorry to be so late." Jed wrote his arrival time on the calendar. His gaze followed the blue car pulling away. "She seems nice. Staying here? Anything special going on I should know about? You look a little glazey-eyed."

"She's Cabin Three. Never you mind my eyes."

But, yeah, she was nice. That wasn't anything he was going to discuss with Jed, though. "A couple of late arrivals scheduled for the weekend and the usual few who'll want directions to the pavilion."

"You going to play up there tonight?"

He hadn't decided yet. As much as he loved live music, being on stage—even the one at the pavilion—was more public than he liked anymore. More open to conversation and loud voices and people's emotions getting away from them. Sometimes it made the PTSD that kept him company on a daily basis hover closer to the edges than was comfortable.

While the campground had given him a much-needed level of peace and quiet, he still had to be aware all the time. Of anyone or anything that might constitute a threat to anyone under his watch. Sometimes it took so little to put him back in the place where he'd landed his disabled helicopter in the middle of a nest of snipers.

He hadn't been hurt—he'd even been commended for setting his helo down without injury to passengers or crew. Personnel had been injured after the landing, though, and two had died. Ez was left with a full ration of guilt. He should have known better than to take it down where he did. Wasn't that why pilots had sixth senses? They were supposed to be more intuitive than most.

He could still hear gunfire.

****

Nearly a year after her divorce was finalized, Joss still wasn't crazy about going to social events by herself. She'd grown used to eating alone in restaurants; having a book in her purse had ensured that she was better read than she'd been since the years of waiting in the car until the boys got out of whatever practice they were in. She actually liked going to the movies alone, because she could go to every chick flick that hit the screen without anyone complaining, plus she had the added incentive of never having to share her popcorn.

The difference hit harder when everyone else in the place seemed to be half of a couple, though, and she was almost sure that was the way it was going to be at the pavilion.

Maybe she wouldn't go.

As she toed off her shoes and booted up her laptop, Allie's words echoed in the back of her mind. *They've won.* "No." Joss slipped her feet back into her shoes and closed the laptop on a crossword she hadn't yet started. "Not today, they haven't."

The pavilion was so crowded she was sure no one would realize she was a woman alone anyway.

Somewhere in the middle of the haphazard semi-circle of chairs that surrounded the stage, a voice called, "Joss! Over here!" Romy was standing and waving.

Gratitude rushed in where trepidation had been. Saying "excuse me" and "so sorry" numerous times, Joss wormed her way through the crowd to take the chair beside Romy. "Thank you for saving me a seat."

"I'm glad you came. This is always a fun time."

Joss looked around, taking in the size of the crowd and its varied demographic. "There are kids here. Teenagers, I mean. Do their friends know they're coming to listen to country music?"

"Some of them even play it." Romy waved a dismissive hand at her. "And it's not all country. Ez has opened it up to any music that's neither profane nor hateful. Of course, there is discussion sometimes because geezers and high schoolers don't exactly see eye-to-eye on what qualifies."

The woman sitting on Joss's other side leaned forward. "We've been coming here ever since the campground opened the first time five or so years ago. Ez buying it is the best thing to happen here since that first day."

"Be even better if he'd get some liquor in here," grumbled a man farther down the row of chairs. "If you don't bring your own, you're out of luck."

Romy turned her head to look directly at Joss and rolled her eyes. "It's a dry county. He couldn't sell it, even if he wanted to."

"He could," the man argued. "He wouldn't have to advertise it, just put it behind the counter there where he keeps his own bottle. He has a lot of vets staying here. They want booze."

Sounds from the stage warned them things were about to begin. Tuning up was cacophonous, punctuated by much laughter and exaggerated groans from the performers. Joss thought of summers past. Being close to tone deaf, she neither played nor sang, but Gray played the drums, Seven the guitar, and June the flute. By summer's end, they'd always sounded good, but the first jam sessions after they arrived at the farm had been much like what was happening on the stage.

The host was a seventy-something man Joss remembered from when she was younger. Wilson DeWitt had lived in Banjo Bend, and she'd been enthralled to see—even from afar—an actual TV star. When she learned he went to school with her father, she was even more excited. His introductory song demonstrated that his voice had mellowed and gentled in the ensuing years.

She exchanged smiles with Romy and relaxed in her chair, looking forward to the performances. She and Brett had watched live music together, but he'd only been interested in headliners, no matter the genre. They'd gone to the Grand Ole Opry often, and she'd loved it, but she'd had more fun visiting small clubs with girlfriends.

The campground's open mic felt much like those evenings had. People sang along. At the end of the rows of chairs, couples danced. At one point, a group gathered in front of one of the fireplaces and line danced. "I'd like to do that someday," she said. "It's always looked like so much fun."

"It is." Romy tucked an arm through hers. "Stick around, Murphy. Living on the creek will all come back to you."

It already was. Joss found a level of comfort in this place that she hadn't felt in a long time. That was an odd thing, since she'd never been a country girl. Even when she was a kid, she knew the idyllic summers weren't real. They were a dream time—a time that made winters of vague discontent more bearable than they would have been otherwise. The carefully chosen clothing her mother sent mostly remained in her suitcase as she ran around in the same three pairs of cutoffs and faded tank tops until time to go back to Dolan Station. The only exception to that rule was the sundresses the girls wore to church on Sundays, which were hung up as soon as they got home.

It had been such a long time since she'd dreamed.

Another group of musicians replaced the ones on stage. Wilson DeWitt covered the transition time by leading the crowd in "I Saw the Light."

The song the new group began with was newer than what had been played earlier in the evening…darker. The lead singer's voice was rough, with an underlying silkiness. The music was fuller and cleaner than had been played by the previous groups. The guitarist was…

Ezra McIntire. That's who it was. Standing away from the front of the stage, not smiling, not looking at the crowd. He seemed to be lost in the music he played. He was still not quite clean-shaven, still growly-looking. But the heathery green sweater he wore looked soft, its sleeves pushed up to his elbows and exposing muscled forearms. His jeans looked as if they'd been made for him, and despite the threads of silver in his dark brown hair, he looked ten years younger than he had earlier.

He looked…spectacular. Her heartbeat did a little dance against her ribs. Heat rushed into her cheeks, and she was prepared to blame a hot flash when Romy's soft murmur reached her ears.

"He cleans up really well, doesn't he?"

Joss saw no point in pretending she didn't know who her friend was talking about. They were both women, after all, and neither of them was dead. "He does."

"He has quite a following." Romy nodded toward the front row, where a group of women swayed to the music. "He never seems to pay attention, although he's always polite to everyone. I don't think anyone on the creek knows him any better than they did the day he came here."

Joss watched him play, rapt by the way his fingers moved over the strings in a sweet flow when he strummed and in complicated rhythm when he picked a lead.

The crowd applauded when his guitar drove the music, but he didn't look up, just went back to strumming.

She thought she knew him, which was craziness in itself—they'd met less than thirty hours before. But she still felt it.

The music lasted until ten o'clock, ending promptly when the musicians played Leonard Cohen's haunting "Hallelujah," joined by quiet voices throughout the shelter.

"I'm off." Romy got to her feet. "I don't work Sundays, but it's a full day anyway. My car's right here. Do you want a ride to your cabin?"

"No, thanks. It's a nice night to walk."

"Well, hey, it was fun."

Romy's smile was so infectious, Joss couldn't imagine anyone not responding to it.

"I go to line dancing on Wednesday nights. If you're still at the campground, drop me a text, and we can go together."

Having a girlfriend to go places with gave her a good feeling. "I'll think about it. Right now, I'm going to sit by that fire a little bit. My granddad isn't here to tell stories, but it's still a nice night for it." Joss meandered through the dwindling crowd to the fire at the end of the pavilion. Someone had already doused the one at the other end, and pushed the picnic tables back into place near it.

She sat in one of the Adirondack chairs that formed a semicircle around the fireplace, nodding a greeting to the young couple who sat a few chairs away. The fire, although it was burning low, was mesmerizing, and she leaned into the curved seat. She wished Sam and Noah were here and that she'd long ago been insistent on bringing them back to this place that was such an important part of who their mother became. As far as they knew, she had no life experience beyond the four-bedroom, three-bath house in Dolan Station.

She guessed that was close to right. Other than summers on Banjo Creek and a year at a college an hour away from home, she'd never lived anywhere besides the suburb. Brett grew up two streets over, and they bought a house in a subdivision comfortably situated near his parents when they got married.

Nothing was wrong with the person she was, even if she did lack life experience. Nothing at all. She'd liked herself as Brett's wife and the twins' mother, as well as the part-time librarian who worked and loved all departments in the Dolan Station branch until her job had suddenly been defunded. She still missed her friends from the book club and the women's group at church and the coffee house on the corner of Fourth and Market.

She'd liked herself because, after all, what was there not to like? She was generous with her time and the money at her disposal, any prejudices she had were kept buried because the last thing on her list of wants was to ever hurt or be unfair to another person, and she could honestly say she found something to like in nearly everyone she'd ever met.

Except that she didn't want to be that person

anymore. Because she didn't like Cassie and Brett or even her mother. She didn't like the woman two houses down in the neighborhood whose language had been laced with racial epithets and cruelties. She didn't like the man who'd insisted he wasn't homophobic at the same time he suggested same-sex couples should be barred from the subdivision.

Not liking those people was perfectly okay. She should have figured that out a long time ago.

Ez took the chair next to hers.

She didn't look his way, but she knew it was him. His music still hummed under her skin. "Do you like pleasers?"

"What?"

"Pleasers. Do you like people who are always nice?"

"Depends."

"That's no answer." She looked at him then, noticing that the young couple had left. She turned her head the other way and realized everyone else had, too. A glance at her watch told her she'd been sitting here longer than she'd realized. The fire was mere coals.

"Sure, it is. If a person hides behind being a pleaser, then, no, I don't like it. It means they're pretending to be something they're not. But if a person's genuinely nice, who am I to question that?"

"It's the genuine part that bothers me. How do you tell?" Ez had the most beautiful eyes. Darker gray than any she'd ever seen, they looked black in the dim light from the dying fire. They were as hard to look away from as the flames had been.

"Depends on if you're looking outside at someone else or inside at yourself. If it's someone else, I don't know—you have to trust your own judgment. If it's yourself, and being a pleaser is making you angry, maybe it's not real." He held her gaze in the flickering light. "Or maybe it's time to please yourself instead of the people around you."

"Is that what you're doing?" She didn't know him well enough to ask these questions, but she asked anyway. No one would remember in the light of day, would they? Even if one was fully sober, confessions before a nighttime fire were things to be forgotten.

"I wouldn't say so."

He spoke a few seconds before the silence had gone on too long.

"Like you before you came here, I needed to be somewhere different than where I was. Gray was there at the right time saying the right thing. A habit of his, I might add."

She drew in the memory, and a chuckle tickled her throat. "It always was. He was the oldest of us. Even when our ages were still single digits, he was our voice of wisdom." As quickly as the laughter had come, tears took its place, thickening her voice. "I loved my life. As silly as it sounds, I thought it would just go on forever. I hate that two years after I found out he and my sister were involved and ten months after our divorce, I'm still not over it. I'm still this whiny person who doesn't know what to do with herself."

Unbelievably, the man beside her laughed. Not just a little, but loudly into the quiet night. When she pushed forward in her chair—being laughed at was the final straw in this horrible moment of vulnerability—he stopped her with a hand on her arm.

"Wait." His voice was soft, the hand gentle.

"Wait."

So she did, not looking at him. He held her arm, his fingers splayed over the fabric of her sweatshirt. The touch was warm and strong, yet still gentle. She didn't want him to take it away. But she didn't want him laughing at her, either.

"Sometimes," he said quietly, "we're all whiny people, and if anyone tells you they always know what to do at any given time in their lives, they're lying."

She was silent for a moment, smiling when the fire popped and sizzled as it died down. "That's true, isn't it?"

"It is. I'm not sure of all that much, but I promise you that's true."

They got up at the same time. He picked up the guitar case beside his chair, and without talking about it, they walked toward her cabin.

"Do you like to line dance?" She shuffled a little sidestep.

"I don't know. I've never tried it. Experience with learning the electric slide tells me I may never want to."

She walked on, thoughtful. The woods whispered around them. Voices came from campsites as people gathered around their own fires. It was a blissful kind of quiet. "About that job."

"What job?"

She sighed. Were all men obtuse, or just the ones she knew? "The one on the bulletin board here and in town."

"Oh, that one. Did you meet someone who wants to apply?"

"Yes." They reached her porch, and she stepped onto it. "Me."

Chapter Four

Ez looked at Joss, not quite believing what she said. He didn't think he was sexist—he'd served with some of the best women anywhere in the military—but Joss wasn't just a girl; she was a girly girl. Her handshake was firm, but the hand itself was soft and the nails carefully kept. She wore makeup, for heaven's sake. She couldn't possibly think she was up to the tasks he'd told her were part of the job. Maybe some of them, but he couldn't see her riding a tractor in front of the mower or snowplow or fighting with the weed whacker. Or unstopping drains. He grinned…he couldn't help it, but he hoped he covered the expression before she saw it. "What do you mean?"

"I can paint as well as anyone. I raised two boys in a house with three bathrooms—I know about plunging toilets. Our lot was an acre and I took care of it myself until the kids were old enough to help—my husband didn't even know how to start the lawn tractor. I know enough about wiring to keep an electrician on speed dial and almost that much about plumbing, but I'm a good gofer."

"Can you pitch a tent for a camper who has no idea what sh…they're doing?"

"I can. Not fast, but I can."

"Can you help someone trying to set up and stabilize a camping trailer?"

"No, but I could learn how."

"Can you work twelve hours if your replacement doesn't show up?"

"Yes." She swallowed hard. "I don't want to, but I can."

"Where will you live?"

"I don't know yet. I'd like to come to some kind of agreement about me staying in Cabin Three for a while." She stopped and cleared her throat. "Or let me stay in the house. I'll work on it in my off time to make up for rent. I think I'd be much more helpful if I lived on the premises."

He hadn't exactly had that in mind. He'd thought maybe a couple of guys in the early stages of retirement or another student or two as young and eager to work as Jed. He hadn't counted on a small woman his own age who smelled like—

Well, this was getting ridiculous, but she smelled really good. "Do you have references?"

"I can get one from the library where I worked and from places I volunteered." She smiled brightly, a fine show of bravado. "If you like, I'll paint the cabin I'm staying in so you can see my work."

He thought of the cabins, of the dingy, off-white paint on all the walls. "It's a deal."

"Only I won't paint the rooms white. Or beige."

He wanted to throw up his hands and say he didn't *care* what colors she chose—he had other things to worry about when it came to making this godforsaken place into one that didn't lose money on a daily basis. He didn't need to be rich, but he wasn't a fan of hunger, either. "After you paint Cabin Three, we'll look at this again, okay? So, you're hired on a trial basis. The pay's abysmal, in case I didn't mention that."

"You did."

"Did I tell you there were no benefits?"

"Yes."

"As long as we're in the off season, you can just stay in an unrented cabin, although not while you're painting it, at least until the house is livable. If you're still here when things pick up in spring, we'll revisit it. Does that work for you?"

She nodded.

"I have an account at the hardware store in Banjo Bend. You can get whatever paint you need there."

"All right."

"No mustard-colored bathrooms." Maybe he did care about paint colors, after all. Her story about her grandfather and the baby poop had kind of resonated. But what was wrong with the pearl gray Ben, the guy from the hardware store who played a mean banjo, had assured him was the new off-white in neutrals? Ez scowled at his newest employee. "Or lavender. No lavender anywhere."

Joss frowned back. "Tell you what. Let me paint the cabin I'm in the way I would choose. If you don't like it, I'll repaint everything with absolutely no character or personality, and I'll pay for the paint. Just give me a chance to add a little…something."

"Deal."

"Would you like me to start tomorrow?"

"There's a church service at the pavilion in the morning. Everyone is invited. Pastors from all around take turns preaching. Afterward, weekend campers start leaving. Retirees and people who live in their motor homes don't keep to the same kind of schedule. If you'd like to come to the office around eleven and learn checkout procedures, then that would be a good start."

"All right. I'll probably come to the service, too. Maybe they'll sing 'In the Garden.' It always starts the week off right for me."

He thought the whole porch lit up when she smiled.

"Goodnight, Ez. I enjoyed your music."

"Goodnight, Joss." He started to walk away, then turned back. "Thank you. It…the music means a lot to me. I'm glad you liked it." He waited to hear the lock on the cabin door click before he turned and sauntered toward the log house beside the creek. Campfires lit the way, and the hushed voices of campers blended with night sounds from the woods. He loved the campground on nights like this. He'd enjoyed playing music and talking with the pretty woman from Cabin Three. The people camping were nearly all repeat guests who knew the rules and pretty much adhered to them, although a couple of them groused about him refusing to sell liquor under the table.

He wasn't sure what had possessed him to hire Jocelyn Murphy. Granted, Margaret could do almost all the jobs on the place, too—including a few he wished she wouldn't—but Joss just looked too…delicate. Yeah, that was the word. He'd bet she wouldn't like it if she knew that's how he looked at her, either.

The thought made him laugh aloud as he went into his house. He took his guitar out of its case and propped it on the stand where it lived, then went into the kitchen to pour a drink, going light on the bourbon. He didn't think his drinking was a problem, but since the possibility had crossed his mind, maybe it was. He liked it better than he liked calling his therapist in the middle of the night during an attack of panic, but he wasn't a fan of any kind of dependency.

He sat on the porch facing the creek with his glass in his hand, wishing he had a dog. While he didn't want any people counting on him to take care of them, he thought even he could keep a dog fed and housed. He remembered Elwood and Jake, the shelties he and his brother had raised. The last time Ez was home, Silas still had dogs from the same bloodline.

Sometimes…oh, God, sometimes he just flat out ached for home, for normalcy, to love and be loved by someone. Occasionally he thought it might be worth the risk. But it wouldn't. He couldn't do that to someone; it would be like selling a car without an engine thinking it might run anyway. He had no engine to offer anyone. Not even a dog.

A gunshot, far away and muffled by the night, echoed from across the creek. Hunters. He flinched. He always flinched. A world of difference lay between the sounds of a sniper attack and a lone shotgun in the deep Kentucky darkness. But memory rode roughshod over his nerves, pushing him back into his chair and making his hand tremble so that the liquid in the glass sloshed close to its rim.

Only this time his mind didn't return to Iraq, but to his classroom in the peaceful town in Virginia where he finished his doctorate and went on to teach statistics at the small private college. He achieved full professorship and started seeing an adjunct who taught in the same building. He and Lucy weren't in love, but they laughed about being seriously in like.

Until the shooter infiltrated the campus. More to the point, his classroom. Ez and a student disarmed and subdued the young man before anyone was hurt, although bullet holes riddled the walls and shattered glass created a lethal hailstorm. Ez was calm that day, and he stayed calm through the ones that followed. The depositions, the conversations with traumatized students, even the journalists who gathered apologetically seeking statements from the hero of the day were within the wheelhouse of what he could handle. Increased dosage of his medication ensured a few hours of sleep each night.

At midterm, he'd had to flunk a kid in his grad level class. Just as he'd had to fail the shooter the semester before. Suddenly he couldn't go back to campus anymore. He took a sabbatical the college was glad to allow him and holed up in his apartment, watching movies on television and playing the same songs over and over again. He broke up with Lucy, although she remained his friend even when he completely failed at being hers.

That was when Gray told him about the campground. It took less than two weeks to complete the transaction that made it home. His safe place. At least, he hoped so.

Another gunshot accelerated his heartbeat, and he drained the glass. Time to go inside, to pour another drink and play music loud until his soul calmed down. Maybe a break would come in the nighttime tunnel of despair, a respite that would allow him to sleep.

In the house, he sat in front of the floor-to-ceiling windows with his guitar. He strummed and picked, then stopped the vibration of the strings with the palm of his hand, straining to hear the gunshots he knew were out there. Then he played "In the Garden," humming when he forgot many of the words. Eventually there was peace…and sleep. And he didn't have another drink.

****

Joss enjoyed the checking-out procedure. It reminded her of the library. She liked that Ez sent the campers on their way with to-go cups full of free drinks and a semi-friendly, "Take care now." When it was her turn to check someone out, she added, "Thanks for spending time with us. See you next time."

Ez rolled his eyes.

She ignored him and went into the store side of the building. He might know his business better than she did, but she understood hospitality. If she hadn't learned anything else at her mother's society-conscious knee, she'd learned that. "You need a library in here." She straightened shelves, checking expiration dates as she went and pushing the freshest dairy items to the back of the cooler.

"A library?"

"Yes. Shelves where people can leave a book and take a book. Or just take one, for that matter. Not all campers want to fish and hike or even sit around the fire. Some of them just want to read where it's quiet and no one wants them to do anything."

He stood in the doorway between the office and the store. "Where would you put this library? It's pretty full in here."

"Here." She pointed to a display of insect repellent and tanning lotion. "No one's tanning now, so you could just put that in the back room somewhere. The repellent needs to be in the office. That space would be plenty for a nice bookshelf. You could even have CDs and DVDs if people who still use them wanted to put them there."

He leaned against the doorframe. "And what's the financial purpose in all this?"

The charcoal in his plaid shirt matched his eyes and made the silver in his hair stand out. Wonderfully. "What?" She needed to pay more attention to the conversation and less to what Ez looked like—that was obvious.

"Money," he said patiently. "How does this pay off for the business?"

"Oh, well—" She stared at the bottles of tanning lotion. Things had always come back to money with Brett, too. No matter how much they had, it was never enough. She always figured his tendency toward acquisitiveness came from him being a banker.

No matter how unfair it might be, she was disappointed the handsome man in the flannel shirt was worried about his bottom line, too. "It probably doesn't, except that while a person's in here to get a book, she might buy something. I would. I have several books we could start with." She heard the resentment in her own voice and knew she had no right to it. She shook her head. Who did she think she was? "Or we—"

"I have some, too. I usually donate them to the VA Hospital in Lexington, but I could put them here. At least some of them."

That was more like it. "There's an empty bookshelf in the house. May I paint that and use it? I'm sure it would fit here."

He shrugged. "Fine with me. I'll move it down here whenever you're ready."

"What will I be doing tomorrow?"

"Painting one of the unoccupied cabins. Probably

Seven." He held up a forestalling hand. "If I need you up here, I'll call."

"Okay."

"And, while we're talking about it, as we agreed, you can stay in the cabin as long as we don't need it, but here's the key to the house. That way, if you have downtime you want to spend doing stuff there, you can. As soon as it's ready for appliances and as much furniture as you need, you can move in there."

She took the brass key he proffered. The engraving on its head reached her heart, making its beat trip over itself. It was her grandmother's initials. "Thank you."

They talked about what hours she would work and what he expected from her. She both appreciated and worried about the latitude he offered.

When Jed, one of the part-time workers, arrived at noon, he and Joss introduced themselves while Ez took most of the contents out of the cash drawer. He left extra change. "A bunch of retirees from Louisville will be checking in this afternoon. Their annual fishing trip. They'll probably buy supplies. If you want to close up and take off after they get here, that's fine. Just put the sign on the door with the number on it."

Jed stepped behind the counter to count the change. He nodded agreement.

Joss and Ez left the office together. The UTV sat outside the office, but when she started toward her cabin, Ez fell into step beside her. "You drove down here," she reminded him.

"I know, but the vehicle stays here in case it's needed by whoever's minding the office and the store." He looked around, the cool breeze sweeping back the thick hair on his forehead. "Would you—" He stopped.

She lifted her gaze to meet his. "Would I what?"

"Would you like to have dinner tonight? It's still nice enough to grill outside, so I could cook a couple of steaks and baked potatoes." He smiled, warmth filling the creases in his face

She couldn't have looked away if her life depended on it. She thought of the hamburger patty she had left over from the night before and decided a steak and potato sounded pretty good. "I'll bring dessert."

"Great. You know where the house is, right?"

She nodded. She'd seen it the morning before when she'd walked around the campground. It was beautiful—all logs and windows and porches set in strategic places.

"About six-thirty okay?"

"Perfect." She didn't think he was any more comfortable asking her to join him for dinner than she was accepting, but something was exciting about the idea of sharing a meal with an attractive man she wasn't married to. She shouldn't be so surprised. Divorced women dated all the time. She'd survived—at least vicariously—the "starting over" phase with more than one girlfriend. She'd seen Cassie do it after the endings of three marriages.

Now her sister was on her fourth, to the only man Joss had ever been in love with.

She let herself into her cabin, her reluctant mind on Cassie and Brett. She thought of Sam and Noah and wondered anew how her mother had always so easily chosen her older child over her younger one. Granted, Cassie had been prettier, looking more like their mother's side of the family, but still.

Yes, still.

This whole lifetime later, long years after she'd grown accustomed to being the also-ran in the race between the Murphy girls, it still hurt.

She took a shower and washed her hair, feeling sticky after working in the store that morning. Being productive was fun, though, and she couldn't wait to get started brightening things up. The thought stopped her in her tracks. Brett had always been annoyed by her proclivity for color. Was it a guy thing? Would Ez hate her ideas as much as her husband had?

Speaking of color, what should she wear to Ez's? Her travel wardrobe didn't extend to dressing for dinner dates. This wasn't a date. She wasn't sure of much right now, but she was positive of that. And why had she offered to take dessert? It wasn't as if she had a full pantry to choose from.

But she did have what it took to make apple crisp. She might have to cheat a little, but it wouldn't be the first time anyone had made the recipe without lemon juice.

Allie called while the dessert was in the oven, and she sat at the table to talk, sipping on a cup of Earl Grey. It made the day—at least for twenty minutes or so—a kind of normal that was sustenance unto itself.

Later, as she across the campground, she didn't feel normal at all. She had to ring the doorbell with her elbow, since her hands were full of still-hot baking dish, and stepped back in surprise when the door swung open immediately.

The thought that he'd been waiting gave her a nice little burst of pleasure.

He took the apple crisp and led the way through the comfortably furnished house.

"It's a pretty house." She wondered who'd furnished it, because whoever it was had spent some time with color and texture. The warmth of the interior design was palpable. As large as the great room was, it was both cozy and inviting, albeit in an impersonal way.

He looked around. "It is, isn't it? Much bigger than I need. I think the guy who built it was going to make it a rental, but bankruptcy interrupted his plans."

"Are you going to?"

"Going to what?"

"Make it a rental."

"No." Surprise showed on his face as soon as he said the word.

She wondered if he'd made the decision without realizing he'd done it. That was something she could identify with. "What are your plans for the campground?"

"To keep it going without it becoming too much of a money pit. There's privacy here. Quiet. It seems that people who camp all the time are both social and respectful of personal space. I like that." He took a platter holding two steaks out of the refrigerator. "Do you want to come outside while I do this?"

"Sure." She held the door for him to go onto the deck off the kitchen. "So, what do you like best? The social part or the respect for personal space?" She thought she knew, but she wanted to hear what he had to say about it.

He didn't answer right away, tossing the steaks onto the hot grill and pushing them into place. "Personal space," he said finally. "Other people being social—I like that, too. I like to watch them having a good time. But it's like playing music. I'm okay onstage as long as I'm at the back. I'll even sing, but not up front."

"How long were you in the military?"

"Twenty years."

"Where did you grow up?"

"Missouri."

"You didn't want to go back there?"

"I did go back."

The one-word answers and the intensity in the last one told her he wouldn't welcome more questions. She went to the rail of the deck and leaned her elbows on it. "You have a wonderful view here."

"I do."

She spoke into the silence. Not that she was one of those people who had to have conversation all the time, but if he hadn't asked her here so they could get to know each other, exactly what had been his purpose? "Do you have any kids?"

"No. How do you want your steak?"

"Medium. I have two. Twins who are twenty-four. Their dad expected them to follow him into the bank and instead, Sam is a high school basketball coach, and Noah is a winemaker. They spent the last summer while they were in college working at a friend's winery in Oregon, and they never really came home again."

"Was that hard? Having them go so far away?"

Unexpected tears flooded her eyes. "It still is."

Going west was her first planned course of action when she decided to leave Tennessee—she still had the route to the Oregon town where her sons lived programmed into her GPS—but the very last thing she ever wanted to do was become her children's responsibility.

"When it was me, I was glad to go." Coldness had replaced the previous sound of his voice.

She did turn then. "They were, too." She rubbed her left thumbnail with her right one, giving the activity far more attention than it deserved. "I guess I was pleased for them that they were making their dreams come true, but I still didn't want them to go. Their dad was disappointed that neither of them wanted to join him at the bank, but mostly he didn't want them to go, either." She grinned suddenly, surprised when it didn't hurt. "On the other hand, he was ecstatic when I left."

He smiled back at her, although his eyes remained dark and solemn.

"Why?" She hoped she wasn't risking her dinner by being nosy—she was hungry. "Why were you glad to go?"

"These will be done in just a minute. I forgot to bring out the plates. Will you get them off the counter?"

She went inside, coming back with the two brightly colored plates that had been on the island in the kitchen. "I'm impressed. Orange and turquoise plates." His smile looked more genuine than it had before.

He put the meat on the plates and handed her one. "My mother had them when I was a kid. She felt about color the way you do. I don't know what happened to hers, but I saw these online and ordered them."

"I had them, too. The boys took them out west. Sam says women like them. Noah says they break too easily."

They worked together in the kitchen. She took sour cream and butter from the refrigerator while he got the potatoes out of the oven.

"I was glad to go"—he poured red wine into glasses and handed her one—"because I was one of those who thought the grass was always greener on the other side of the fence. I had to be shown, over and over, that it wasn't really greener there—it was just the other side."

She sipped the wine as they went to the table. "This is good." She didn't know why she was surprised, but she was. The bottomless glass of bourbon and soda he usually had with him had probably led her opinion of his wine expertise.

"Don't be too impressed. Margaret's my wine person. She decrees that if it's on sale on the end cap at the supermarket, it's good."

Joss purchased wine the same way—she didn't see it as a problem. "Who's Margaret?"

"She came with the campground. If I'm not here to answer any questions you have, she's the one you'll ask. She knows more about the place than anyone."

Their conversation wasn't easy, although it was friendly. Joss was afraid she'd go too far with curiosity. Too much time had passed since she'd talked to men as anything but a married woman. Even after her divorce, she'd been Brett's ex. She'd forgotten about being just herself.

Whoever that was.

"One of my boys always chases the greener grass." She scooped apple crisp for dessert as Ez put their dinner plates into the dishwasher. "The fact that his twin holds his coat while he climbs the fence made raising them a real adventure."

Ez stopped moving.

A look of longing crossed his face, so fast she

thought she might have imagined it.

"Do they get along?"

"Oh, yeah. They even did a paper once in high school on being twins. They dressed alike—which they've never done—and switched back and forth with the presentation. Then the people watching had to say which kid was which. I was glad I wasn't there. They might have fooled me, too. Not for long, but they could have done it. When Noah said he wanted to go to Oregon, we knew Sam would be looking for a job there."

"How often do you see them?"

She set their dessert plates on the table. He followed with coffee.

"A few times a year. If there's a cheap flight, they'll come in for a long weekend. I went out for a few days when the high school where Sam coaches and teaches was on spring break." She smiled. "Even when your kids are in their twenties, they don't like it when their parents get divorced. They needed to see that I was okay with it."

He laid down his fork. "Were you?" He caught and held her gaze.

She couldn't look away, and she couldn't tell less than the truth. "Oh, Lord, no, but they didn't need to know that." She sipped coffee from the heavy turquoise cup, enjoying the richness of the brew. It might keep her awake later, but the memory of the flavor would make it worth it. "Somewhere between then and now, it became true. I really am all right most of the time."

"Happy?" A lifted eyebrow lent skepticism to his look.

She hadn't expected him to ask that, although she

couldn't have said why. Perhaps because she was almost sure he was anything *but* happy. "Not really." She kept her voice quiet and emotionless. "I'm not at all certain happiness isn't an illusion at the best of times. Or, if it's not an illusion, I don't think it's something you can hold onto. It's like butterflies—really pretty and nice, but short-lived."

****

Ez walked Joss back to her cabin after they'd shared dessert and coffee. He wasn't just using the manners his mother had taught him, he realized—he wanted to spend more time with his newest employee.

While he wasn't prepared to enter into a relationship with any depth to it, talking with someone about things other than the campground was nice. He missed the college and his friends from there, but that part of his life still felt like a huge and throbbing bruise. His military career was more like a dream than the twenty years of learning and teaching and doing it had been.

It was as if—and the thought made him laugh out loud as he walked back to his house alone in the dimly lit night—he'd been born when he came to the shabby property on Banjo Creek. In a way, he supposed he had, but the wounds planted on his soul by the past were still waiting in the woods to go on the attack.

He wondered if Joss was right about happiness. He'd always thought it was out there somewhere, even if it had eluded him. Maybe it wasn't. Maybe it had to be created.

The house was too quiet when he got back. He played his guitar for a while, emptied the dishwasher, and poured a couple of fingers of bourbon to help him sleep. He thought about Silas. They hadn't really talked in so long. He didn't think his brother ever forgave him for leaving the farm when their father needed him to stay. No matter how much money Ez sent home, it had never made up for the fact that he wasn't there and had no intention of returning. He'd covered all the costs insurance hadn't when Pop had to go into a memory care nursing home, but Silas had been the one who'd visited almost every day.

Silas had always been the good son.

Were Joss's sons that way? The good one and the bad one? He doubted it. He thought she was more like his mother had been. The old man had never left anyone in doubt about his preferences, but if Mom had favorites, no one ever knew it.

He should call Silas, just to make sure he was all right, or at least text him. His brother hadn't married again after he and Jackie divorced, which was a surprise. Si was the marrying kind. Loyal and diligent. The good son in every way.

Ez realized he was making his brother sound like a German shepherd and flinched inwardly. Once when they were arguing, Si had shouted that he *wasn't* man's best friend, using a few expletives in the process. Then he'd stomped out of the room, going off on his own to do the right thing because that was what he always did.

The phone vibrated at his elbow, and he picked it up, looking at the screen.

—*U doing ok?*—

He stared at the words for a moment. How strange was that? Nothing intuitive flowed between him and his brother. They'd tolerated each other all the years they lived in the same house. They'd both dated the same girl in high school, but when Jackie chose Si, Ez walked away with very little comment. They'd never wished each other harm—at least, Ez didn't think they had. He didn't think they'd given each other much thought at all.

And yet. Here was that text, sent within minutes of…well, it was just weird, was all.

—*Good. U?*—

—*OK*—

And that was it. The McIntire brothers' conversational efforts were nothing if not succinct. He started to refresh his drink, but put down the bottle instead.

It had been a good day.

Chapter Five

"Bring any of it in you want to. We'll put in some color and shake it up for you. It was all bought here anyway."

Three days into her first week as a campground employee, Joss knew all the employees of Banjo Bend Hardware by name. Ben, the man behind the paint counter, looked familiar. Almost everyone in town did, at least the ones she'd come in contact with. "Did I know you?" she asked. "When I was a kid, I mean?"

"If you were one of the Murphy cousins, probably, but in those days, I didn't talk to girls, so I couldn't say for sure." He bagged her purchases, dropping a few stirrers and a promotional trim brush into the sack. "If you're back to stay, welcome. Your grandparents would be happy about that, I reckon. Have you seen Marley yet?"

"I'm going there next."

"Well, then." He walked around to the colors display and pulled out several cards. "Give her these. Tell her they're new shades we got in just for her. She does love her colors."

She always had. The victim of an early childhood accident that had left her with numerous limitations, Marley's artistic eye was flawless. The group home where she lived was on an old street on the side of town farthest from the creek. The big, square house sat in the center of a lot surrounded by wrought iron fencing.

Joss parked in front of the house and sat for a moment. Would Marley recognize her? Why hadn't she kept in touch, regardless of Brett's and her mother's thoughts on the matter? The cousins had been so close when they were young; why had they allowed adulthood and its demands to sever relationships, or at least reduce them from solid lines to spotty ellipses?

She gathered the paint sample chips and the sketch pad and crayons she'd brought and got out of the car.

An attendant answered the door, closing it as soon as Joss was inside. "A couple of residents are too fast for me sometimes," she admitted, "especially on pretty days like this one. Are you here to see Marley? She was so excited when we told her you were coming."

"I'm glad." Joss had to blink to keep from bursting into tears. "I haven't seen her for so long, and I should have. I should—"

"She'll just be happy to see you now." The woman's smile was both forgiving and inviting. "She'll be glad to see those color chips, too. Did Ben send them?"

"He did."

"Come with me."

Joss followed the woman to a sunroom at the back of the house. The room was empty except for one person sitting at a table by one of the walls of windows. She was concentrating fiercely on the drawing in front of her. Her hair, silver now instead of blond, was still in the pixie style she'd worn as a child. Her eyes, when she looked up, were the same clear and guileless blue.

"Jossie." She clasped her hands in delight. "You didn't come yesterday."

She hadn't had many words then, and Romy said she still didn't, but the ones she had were clear.

Joss bent to hug her, breathing in the scent that had always been uniquely Marley's. "I know. I'm late again. I'm sorry. What are you drawing? Rainbows? They're so beautiful."

It had always been rainbows with Marley. Her drawings reflected her love for color, and always somewhere on the page would be a rainbow. Much of her development had plateaued at kindergarten level, but her artwork was strikingly beautiful.

The afternoon flew by. Joss sat with Marley. She read to her from Beatrix Potter books, did her nails, and put lipstick on her each time she asked. She told her where June was every ten minutes or so and sang "Put the Lime in the Coconut" with her. If anyone else came in as they sang, they joined in. Joss was humbled to realize once again that her voice was easily the worst no matter who else was in the room. She met the other three residents of the house and rejoiced in the friendship between the four women.

When Marley was tired, the attendant appeared as if from nowhere. "She rests before supper." She smiled down at her charge. "But she's a happy girl, aren't you?"

"No. I'm Marley." The blue eyes lit with joy, and she pointed at the caregiver. "You're Irene."

"Right you are. Are you going to tell your company goodbye?"

"Not company." Marley beamed. "She's Jossie. She'll be back tomorrow."

"Right." Joss kissed her cheek and smiled a farewell at Irene. Time had made changes in her cousin since she'd seen her, but the sweetness was still the same.

Darkness had fallen by the time she parked in front of her cabin. She was tired—she'd started painting at seven o'clock that morning—but she felt enlivened, too. Such a long time had passed since she'd been productive. Or at least, what she considered productive, and the last three days had filled the well in that part of her soul.

Carrying a flashlight and the paint for the bathroom, she walked down the curvy campground road to Cabin Five. The second coat was on, and she wanted to see how the new colors looked under artificial light.

Inside, she turned on the lights as she walked through the small rooms. With each flipped switch, she grew more delighted. Coming up with a combination that was both bright and conservative, soft without being girly, and warm without being dark had been fairly difficult. She didn't know yet how she would paint the cabins that were geared more toward sportsmen than families, but she'd come up with something.

By the time she returned to the living-dining area of the cabin, she was doing a little dance of self-congratulations. If Ez didn't like these colors, something was obviously wrong with him.

Footsteps sounded on the front porch as she entered the room, followed by a knock on the door. She frowned in consternation. He hadn't rented Seven out, had he? He'd assured her it was empty until the weekend.

When she opened the door, her landlord was on the

other side. He looked relieved to see her. "I couldn't figure out who was here." She stepped back from the door.

He came in, stopping to look around.

"Go ahead." She gestured toward the cabin's interior. "It's all done but the bathroom, which is still river-mud brown. Let me know what you think."

He was back in a few minutes, his thumb raised in a symbol of approval. "It looks great."

"Really?" She felt like an elementary-school cheerleader who'd just been recognized by the varsity captain, a comparison that shocked her all the way to her never-a-cheerleader bones. "So I can keep doing this? The colors will be different, and I'll keep them male and boring for the ones on the other side if you like."

"Use whatever you like. Some of the people who come here need more than a campground is able to provide. Word gets around, you know, that this is a safe place, a welcoming place, and veterans come. Not just them, but others who need to just be away from everyday life. The colors add something to the experience."

She had noticed at the pavilion that night how many people even she could have pinpointed as military, although she couldn't have guessed whether their service was past or present. "That's very hard for you, isn't it?" She carried the day's purchases into the mud-colored bathroom.

"What?" He sounded alert. "What's hard for me?"

She came back into the room and met his gaze, absorbing the pain in it. "People needing things from you."

He didn't answer right away, turning to give the scrambled furniture much more attention than it deserved. "If this is ready to put back, I'll help you with it."

"Okay."

The living area was small and scantily furnished. Moving the couch and chair and dining table and its two chairs was done in a few minutes. "The floors are nice in the cabins," she said, looking down at the oak laminate as raptly as he had the furniture.

"Thank you. We did all of them first. The previous owner had already bought the flooring and stored it in the restaurant building."

"They're great."

He nodded.

Silence created a veil between them. Joss sighed in frustration. She'd thought they were at least becoming friends. They'd talked and laughed a lot over the days since she'd arrived, and the truth of the matter was that she was attracted to him in ways not defined by friendship.

However, she wasn't ready to go there, especially since she wasn't at all sure he shared her interest. She reached for the jacket she'd laid across the chair. "Well, I'm done for the day. I'll do the bathroom tomorrow, unless you had something else you wanted me to do." She asked him that every day, but so far he hadn't assigned anything.

"Actually, would you mind helping Margaret in the store? It's take-in day for supplies. She says she doesn't need help, but she does."

"Of course." They left the cabin at the same time, and Ez walked with her toward Three as she'd known he would. As safe and well-lit as the area was, it was beyond him to let a woman walk alone in the dark.

"You're right. It's not hard that they need things, but that I might not be able to deliver." He spoke abruptly, his voice strained, the words slow and yet sharp.

The pain evident in his eyes back in the cabin was a palpable presence between them as they walked. She wondered what caused it. What had brought him to this place in the most rural part of Kentucky? Was it an oasis to him as it was to her, or was it a punishment? "None of us can deliver all the time." Her words were as slow as his, but measured. She wanted to offer acknowledgment of his concern, but she didn't feel qualified to give succor to the pain that had no name. At least, not a name she knew.

"No."

His teeth gleamed in an unexpected smile that she knew without being able to see didn't reach his eyes.

"But sometimes the failures are ones you can't get over."

She nodded. "I'm sure that's true."

They approached the dark porch of her cabin. "Your light's out. I'll put a new one in in the morning."

"Thank you." How stilted she sounded. Not cheerleader-like at all. More like the kids who'd worked in the library. What was she thinking? She'd worked at a library more years of her life than she hadn't, counting the years in high school. No wonder she sounded like she did. The idea made her laugh aloud, and she realized they really were friends, new ones, feeling their way. That was all. "Do you like BLTs?" She opened the door. "I'm cooking."

"They sound good." His answer was instant. "Would you like me to go grab a bottle of wine?"

"I have one. If you can overcome in a battle with a corkscrew, I'll be glad to share."

He chuckled, the sound rolling over her so that she smiled in response. "That's one battle I can win."

****

Even when he'd shared meals and companionship and physical intimacy with Lucy, Ez didn't recall feeling the way he did sitting across Cabin Three's small round table from Joss.

"Tell me about Missouri." She forked a bite of the coleslaw she'd bought at the cafe. "I've been there, to the Lake of the Ozarks and to St. Louis, but never for long."

He thought about it for a minute, reaching for the bottle of wine and replenishing their glasses. He wondered abstractedly if she'd brought her own wineglasses to the cabin—he didn't think they'd been in the cupboard.

Somewhere between the wine and the wondering came the longing, sharp and sustained. For home, to see Silas, not that they ever had that much to say to each other; it would just be good to see him. "It's beautiful. I grew up on a farm—a bigger one than this, but with woods and a creek running through it much like here. It's about an hour from the Lake of the Ozarks. My brother still lives there."

He stopped for a moment, holding up the stemless glass and swirling its contents. "When we were in high school, we got so tired of mowing the hill behind the house—it was a bear—that we talked the old man into letting us plant grapes. We studied everything about

70

growing grapes all winter, saved money to pay for things ourselves, and created a nice little vineyard."

"Do you get homesick?"

Like right now, for instance? It gnawed at his stomach, and he took another bite of his sandwich, hoping to give it ease. "Sometimes, but I've been gone from there for over thirty years. Nothing I miss is still there." He lifted one shoulder in a shrug. "Well, the grapes. I did enjoy the grapes."

"Your brother is still there. Do you have other family?"

"He has three kids. The oldest two are married, the youngest one being the family adventurer." He thought of pretty Mary and of Davis, who was the image of his father. And of John Ezra, named after Ez. He'd always given Jackie credit for that, but he wondered twenty years later if it had been Silas's idea all along.

"Noah would have liked to have had grapes, but it didn't coincide with subdivision or his father's rules." Joss smiled. "So he became a winemaker instead."

She had a look in her eye that Ez had noticed was a mom thing. "Were you disappointed?

"Surprised, but not disappointed. I'm sure Brett was, but in all fairness, he was a product of his raising. He was everything his parents expected him to be, and he thought Sam and Noah would respond in the same way." She laughed. "Sam always said he might have, but someone needed to go along to keep Noah out of trouble."

They finished their meal, and she put their dishes on the cabin's tiny patch of counter and returned to the table with two dessert plates. "Don't give me any credit. This is Romy's chocolate pecan pie. Apple crisp is about the best I can manage in the cabin."

"If you decide to stay…say, for the winter, you should go ahead and move into the house instead of suitcasing it from cabin to cabin. We can get appliances put in and furnish it enough to make you comfortable." He couldn't believe the words that had just come out of his mouth, but he couldn't call them back.

She took a bite of the pie and laid down her fork, then took the last sip from her wineglass and set it down carefully. Precisely.

He liked her hands. They weren't exactly pretty, but she took good care of them. She wore gloves when she worked, even painting. He thought it was funny that her nails were pristine, but she had paint in the ponytail of red curls pulled back in a scrunchie. He'd seen her enough to know she put makeup on every morning, but she didn't replace it when it wore off.

She divided what was left in the zinfandel bottle between their glasses. "Let's talk about that tomorrow. It will give me time to think about it and you time to change your mind, if you need to."

He lifted his glass and she tapped hers against it, her fingers brushing his in the process. There was a moment of stillness, when their eyes met, and he had the sensation of drowning in the blue of hers. "Tomorrow." His voice was husky.

"Tomorrow."

They drank, their gazes still holding. Looking away was one of the harder things he'd done recently, but he accomplished it. He set down his glass. "Thanks for dinner. My turn next time."

She nodded, her eyes brightening.

He had the happy little thought that she was as

affected as he was by…something…he wasn't really sure what. Walking to his house when he left Cabin Three, Ez realized something had changed in the course of the evening. He thought about the blueness of her eyes, the wild curls of her hair, the warm sense of connection when her hand touched his, and wondered if she'd felt it, too. He hoped she had.

At home, he looked at the bottle of bourbon on the counter thoughtfully, finally deciding he didn't need it on top of the wine he'd already consumed. He was reaching a point where he didn't want to need it at all, but he wasn't there yet. Instead, he leaned back in his recliner and turned on the TV, then reached for his phone, thumbing through the messages until he found the one he was looking for. He studied it for a moment, then tapped the phone's keyboard.

—*Remember the year we started the grapes? It was one of the best years ever.*—

Three dots showed him Silas was answering, and Ez waited.

—*Yeah. It was.*—

Chapter Six

"Mercy sakes." Joss looked at the check-in log on the last Thursday in October. "No wonder you wanted me out of Cabin Three. I didn't realize every single cabin and campsite would be full. Don't these people know it's almost winter?"

"Don't you know it's Halloween weekend?" Ez spoke from where he was replenishing the cooler on the store side. "Hayrides and tricking or treating and storytellers in the pavilion instead of musicians. It's a hot time in the old town…well, the cold campground—or so they tell me. It's my first time, too. It sounds like a throwback to another era."

"It's more fun than you can shake a stick at." Margaret dusted the shelves. "It gets noisy, and there'll always be some teenagers rabble-rousing, but you'll like it." She tossed her head. "As far as being a throwback, young man, many of the best things are."

"I did know there was stuff going on—I just didn't anticipate how much. June's bringing Marley out for a hayride and to watch the trick or treaters." Joss was anxious to see Marley's older sister. She was Sister June Esther now and had been for years, but she'd assured Joss over the phone that just June would still do just fine.

"No June Bug, though." Laughter rang through her voice. "I don't answer to that one anymore."

"You can use the utility vehicle or a golf cart to take them wherever they want to go. Marley's ridden on them before—she likes them," said Ez. "I rented a couple of extras for the weekend, too, so one will be available." He grinned at Margaret. "I was forewarned, therefore forearmed. All the part-timers are working this weekend, so you two have it off." He raised a hand as if to forestall any protests. "They wanted to work—I didn't make anyone do it. Jed says the storytelling alone is worth the effort."

"Oh, it is." Margaret, who was replenishing the books on the shelf she'd just dusted, smiled at Joss, although a faraway look softened her eyes. "Your dad could tell a story. Do you remember?"

"I do." The memory came over Joss with a rush that almost brought tears to her eyes. "He never used a book—he'd just tell them right out of his head. Mother would get mad because he'd get us too excited to go to sleep, but it was worth it." How they felt about their father was one of the few things Joss and Cassie agreed on. Neither of them quite understood how he could love them both the same when their mother couldn't, but he had.

Meeting Margaret had been one of Joss's favorite experiences since coming to the campground. Hearing about her father from someone outside the family gave her a whole new perspective of him.

"I'm going to ride around and do a last-minute check on things." Ez put a jacket on over his flannel shirt. "You want to ride along while we have Miss Margaret here to guard the ramparts?"

"Sure." Joss, who'd replenished her fall wardrobe slightly on a girlfriends' trip to Prestonsburg with

Romy, reached for her own jacket. "You do realize it's cold outside, right?"

"Not to a farmer's kid, it's not." He grinned. "You city kids have no idea what it's like in the real world."

She rolled her eyes. "You caught that, right, Margaret? Does growing up in Banjo Bend instead of on a farm make you a city kid, too?"

The older woman laughed, her eyes twinkling behind her glasses. "To him, it does. I've caught it before. Just throw it back—that's all it deserves."

"Are you going to close for the winter?" Joss climbed into the right side of the utility vehicle for the ride to the campsites.

"We'll open for weekends, weather and reservations permitting, although we won't offer any programs then. Just the office will be open for checking in and out. The store will be open, too, but no perishables. The part-timers are lining up for the hours." He drove slowly through the tent sites, waving at a few regulars setting up their camps.

Joss waved, too, recognizing the people and finding pleasure in it.

"This part will be closed altogether." He waved an encompassing arm around the tent sites. "Not that there aren't people who will tent camp in the cold, but I'd rather they don't do it on my watch. Some of the tent regulars have rented cabins just so they can spend some weekends here. It's a real compliment to the place."

"Do you allow hunters in during closed times?"

"No." His answer was abrupt, not inviting further questions on that particular subject.

"How about fishing?"

He hesitated. "The property's posted against

trespassing, so in a way, no. However, boats tie up at the campground's pier. Fishermen use the few picnic tables that are left out in the pavilion. We leave one set of restrooms unlocked, and they use them. So far, there's been no abuse of the privileges. If there is, we'll have to see."

The pavilion was ready for use, chopped wood stacked neatly under cover at each end. Halloween decorations and strands of orange lights festooned from the ceiling created a holiday atmosphere—or would after dark. "I love the pavilion," said Joss. "Gran talked Granddad into building it when the tobacco barn was torn down. They'd love that it's been enlarged and is still used for so many different things."

Ez's forehead creased, and he ran his fingers over the scruff on his cheek. "How do you think they'd feel about the campground?"

"I'm not sure about that. Gran would like it. She liked anything that meant company was coming. But Granddad loved his farm. He worked in the coal mine to keep it going, even though I guess it never amounted to much." She thought of the summers, of the cousins, of the long table in the kitchen, and couldn't stop either the longing or the sigh it pushed out. "To us kids, this place was everything. To all of us, I think, at different times."

They eased past the cabins, staying out of the way of arriving campers. The cottage exteriors wouldn't be painted until spring, but Joss, Margaret, and Romy spent a Sunday afternoon making autumn wreaths for all the doors. Joss, with Jed's help, painted all the porch rockers on one sunny afternoon, emptying every partial can of spray paint in the storage room.

"I like what you're doing."

Today wasn't the first time he'd voiced approval of her work, but Joss heard extra warmth in his voice. Or maybe she just wanted to. "If I can get the rooms in the house all painted, can I have a family Thanksgiving?" She didn't know where the words had come from. Who was going to show up, for heaven's sake? Her sons were clear across the country, her sister married to Brett, and her mother would never voluntarily come to Banjo Creek.

But maybe the cousins would come. At least, June and Marley. Maybe Gray. She doubted she'd even be able to find Seven, much less persuade him to come. "I'd like you to come, too, and maybe Margaret. I have the impression she doesn't have family around here."

"I don't think she does. Yeah, if you'd like to use the house for that, go ahead. It can be a test run on using it as a B & B or a vacation rental. What do we need to do to furnish it for more people, though?"

He'd already bought new appliances for the house and footed the bill on things she'd brought in from estates sales. Attending them was something she'd learned was habit-forming. He'd helped her move her things in when Allie and her husband brought the contents of her storage unit.

"Mattresses."

"We can do that."

They drove to his house, parking and staring out over the calm water of the creek. "When we were in high school, we used to sit here at night and talk about what we were going to be when we grew up."

"Did your dreams come true?"

"Mine did." For the first time in several weeks,

hurt made her stomach clench. Her fingers, suddenly cold, grasped each other in her lap, her right thumb pinching down on her left so that her knuckle shone white. "My life went exactly as I mapped it out. I did plan on more children, but that didn't happen." Tears pushed against the backs of her eyes, and she stared straight ahead, willing the calm surface of the water to lend its serenity to the twist of pain that threatened to turn her back into the weeping, regretful victim she'd been when she left Tennessee.

Ez's hand, large and warm, rested on hers. He didn't say anything, didn't even squeeze her tortured fingers, but his touch gave her the sense of equanimity she needed. Without meaning to—at least she didn't think she meant to—she leaned just far enough toward him to absorb the comfort his presence provided.

She cleared her throat. "Gray wanted to be Wilson DeWitt. He wanted to make records in Nashville but to make his life here. With whomever the girl of the summer was—it wasn't the one he ended up marrying. I don't know what happened to take him away, but, no, the life he's lived has been unrelated to the one he intended."

"We used to talk about that."

Ez's chuckle was something she felt, rather than heard.

"You learn a lot about people on late nights on navy bases, especially at the bar in the club if you're near the bottom of your third glass of something medicinal."

"Gray's a talker, so I can see that." Joss tilted her head to capture Ez's gaze. "Did he learn things about you, too? That's a little harder to imagine."

79

He didn't answer right away. His hand stayed on hers, clasping gently. "I don't know." He shook his head. "I don't remember who I was then."

The ache in his voice was heartbreaking. She turned her hand to hold his.

"So." He laced his fingers with hers. "What about the rest of you?"

"Marley wanted to live on a rainbow in a little house with a fluffy kitty." Joss smiled, tenderness warm in her chest. "We all wanted to give it to her. June wanted—" She stopped, trying to remember. "I don't know. My aunt and uncle both worked long hours, and June always took care of Marley. I don't remember what her plans were, but I'm sure becoming a nun wasn't one of them."

"There are a couple more of you, aren't there?"

"My sister Cassie and Seven." What was she supposed to say about her sister that didn't make her sound like the victim she so much didn't want to be? "She probably won't be here for Thanksgiving." There, that was enough—he knew the reason. "I don't know where Seven is, but I hope June does."

"Do you and your sister talk?"

"When we forget to be angry, we do." She lifted one shoulder in a rueful shrug. "So, no, not often. The fact that she's married to my former husband just doesn't make for a comfortable relationship."

"My brother and I dated the same girl in high school," he said. "He married her."

"Did you mind?"

He shook his head. "But I always felt like Silas did." He frowned. "I'm not sure how right I was about that."

"Are they still married?"

"No. They've been divorced for probably five years, since their youngest got out of high school."

Joss caught his eye again. "Did she call you after the divorce?" The change in his expression answered the question, but she backtracked anyway. "I'm sorry. That definitely crossed a line."

"She crossed a line, too. So did your sister and your husband."

"They did." The pain came again, less crushing this time. She felt as if she could draw a deep breath. "The boys won't talk to their dad or their aunt. I appreciate them being loyal to me, but at the end of the day, Brett and Cassie love them, and they love Brett and Cassie. Being estranged is just more hurt."

"But it's hurt you're not responsible for. Your kids are adults—they'll have to make peace with the situation on their terms."

He was right. It wasn't anything she hadn't told herself, but hearing it from someone else was nice.

"What were their dreams?"

She had to catch up with their conversation, realizing she'd changed it somewhere in the middle. "Cassie's and Seven's?"

"Yeah. Do you remember?"

"She wanted to be in movies, and she actually was in a few when she was in her twenties. Seven—" She stopped, trying to remember. "He went to Vegas after he got out of the military and became a croupier, but I don't remember if that was his plan or not. He gambled, which Gran worried about, but he never seemed to lose. I think that worried her, too."

Ez chuckled. "I can see why. Getting used to

winning could be dangerous." He took his hand from hers and turned back toward the campground's road.

She felt cold. "What about you?" She tightened her jacket around her body. "What were your dreams?"

"Getting off the farm. I hated it. At least until we planted the grapes. There for a while, I wanted to become a vintner. When I saw that wasn't going to happen, I joined the navy and got to fly helicopters and get an outstanding education. The tradeoff was good for as long as it lasted. So was teaching at the college in Virginia after I retired. At least until—" He stopped abruptly.

The stillness was so chilling she felt as if a wall had fallen between them. Joss sensed he'd said more than he'd intended and searched for something to ask that would make him smile. He had the most beautiful one, all the more so because he didn't use it very often.

"What are—"

"I was thinking—"

They spoke at the same time, fell silent, and started again. "You go." She laughed in sheer relief that the space between them was light again.

"Are you sure?" He laughed, too, then went on. "I was thinking of restoring the restaurant on the property this winter. It wouldn't take much. The structure is solid, and the building isn't that old. Plus, the campground has such a talented paint designer. I could put out feelers and maybe lease it in the spring." He extended a hand in invitation. "Now you."

She grinned. "I was just going to ask if you had plans for the restaurant building." She felt rewarded when he grinned back. By the time they got back to the office, darkness was falling.

Jed had replaced Margaret. "She had a date," he confided. "I reminded her it was a school night and asked if she had her homework done."

Ez chuckled. "Good job, son."

Joss watched them together, remembering the too-seldom and too-brief interchanges between Brett and the twins. He wasn't a bad father, but he wasn't a natural one, either. He was what a divorced friend had referred to as a "wallet daddy." As long as the kids were clean and well-behaved, he was excellent—the messy parts of parenting were what he didn't like.

She had a feeling Ezra McIntire wouldn't have minded the messy parts. The thought left her feeling melancholy. "If you don't need me for anything, I'm going to find a book on the shelf I haven't read and take it home."

She loved living in her grandparents' house. She hadn't started on the upstairs yet, but much of the first floor was what Allie would call Realtor-ready. Joss started finding furniture as soon as Ez suggested she go ahead and move in. While she waited for it to be delivered, she rented a sander and sanded all the hardwood floors. As soon as she'd painted the walls of the rooms, Ez helped her refinish the floors.

Romy, declaring boredom, came to help, too. The following night, Wyatt Iverson, the pastor of the Banjo Bend Community Church, came along with Romy and lent considerable expertise to updating plumbing and wiring. The evening, complete with loud music and pizza, had felt uncannily like the old days with the cousins.

But the house was empty tonight. Just her and memories and a book she couldn't get interested in no matter how hard she tried. Not until she'd showered and dressed in the sweats she wore to bed did she remember the crossword puzzle book she bought on her last trip to Prestonsburg. The volume was coil-bound so that the pages turned easily and lay flat, and the puzzles were difficult, her favorite kind.

Times like these were when she didn't mind being single. Although she still missed Allie and some of the people she'd worked with at the library, she'd acquired a kitchen tableful of friends who kept loneliness at bay. Her life in Dolan Station had receded into what was. Allie's delivery of the contents of her storage unit had severed the last connecting string. Although she still grieved her losses, she'd stopped wishing she could have the old life back…mostly.

She curled into her wing chair, setting a mug of hot chocolate on the table beside her and opening the puzzle book. She put on her favorite green reading glasses and lost herself in a world of big words. Twenty minutes in, she texted Ez for help.

He answered immediately, although his solution was wrong.

She laughed. Peace lay gently in the quiet of the room.

****

Ez was restless. He really wanted to sleep—the weekend would be busy for everyone at the campground. But the redhead up there in her grandparents' house had taken charge of his mind.

It had been so long—he couldn't even have said *how* long—since he'd wanted to actually *share* with someone. Since the word *relationship* had entered his conscious mind. Yet here he was thinking of her, of the wild silkiness of her hair and the laughter in her eyes. He caught himself wondering what color of blue they were. Surely a puzzle clue at some point would tell him, but not so far. They were lighter than sky blue, not as dark as cornflower. When she talked about her kids, they softened to baby blue, but when she laughed, they brightened to...

Was he actually sitting on his porch thinking about the color of a woman's eyes?

The moon, in its third quarter, shone onto the rippling water of the creek. Campers walked past, the sounds of their voices rising and falling as if they were muffled by the smoke from campfires. Faint music from stringed instruments reached him. He knew he could have gone and joined the players—they were regulars—but he wasn't in the mood tonight.

He wanted to go on thinking about the redhead.

The banging started out of nowhere, and he started, leaning forward in his chair. His heartbeat accelerated, and the hair on the back of his neck stood up. It was close. Too close and too loud.

What were those fools doing?

Sweat poured down his sides, cold against his skin inside the flannel of his shirt. His hands shook.

Oh, God, everything shook. The noise went on and on. He looked from side to side, then peered over the porch railing, trying to see what was causing it. Was someone out there intent on doing damage?

He had to go and see what was happening, If necessary, he needed to stop it before someone was hurt. The campground was his to protect. The college kids over in the tent sites. The veterans in the motor homes. Families here, too—parents who homeschooled and could camp long weekends even after school started. One family had foster kids in addition to their own and traveled in an old school bus with the seats taken out and bunks put in—little Jericho was in a wheelchair. He was the funniest little guy. How could Ez keep him safe if some lunatic was out there shooting?

Firearms weren't allowed here, but people brought them in anyway. Ez didn't like it, but he wasn't going to search every vehicle that checked in. That wasn't the kind of safety people were looking for on Banjo Creek. Usually folks were respectful. They only carried their guns because that's what they did—they never shot them. But—

The noise. Oh, the hellacious, endless noise.

He went inside, shaking all over, and got his handgun. What if he had to use it? He was an expert marksman, but his hands were trembling too much to even hope for accuracy. Plus they were wet. Clammy.

When he'd been armed in the military, he'd always been able to separate the job from himself. When he'd had to shoot, it had been to protect himself and others. He'd felt little guilt until after Iraq, when he'd been unable to fulfill what he saw as his duty. People had died—maybe not because of him, but because he hadn't been fast enough. Sharp enough. Accurate enough. The sniper had done so much damage before Ez was able to stop him. So much damage.

The banging continued. Not guns, his mind finally assured him, but fireworks. More popping than cracking. Not as sharp or as carrying, even with the water out there magnifying the sound.

Probably.

He went back to the porch. If he stayed closer to whatever was happening, he'd be better able to identify it. The noise still sounded like fireworks—there was a lack of depth in the reverberation. No echo. Of course, you didn't always hear an echo. You didn't know what was coming at all. But sometimes you felt it. Sensed it. Dreaded it. Smelled it.

And sometimes you flew your chopper right into it. Other times the door of your classroom opened unexpectedly and your lecture on identifying outliers was punctuated with a hail of bullets. The horror of that particular irony matched the day he knew he couldn't fly helicopters anymore. He'd run from teaching as dedicatedly as he'd run from flying. When Lucy came to Banjo Creek to visit, she called it the ends of the earth. He'd been good with that.

The incessant popping and the whistle of rockets went on and on until he didn't think he could bear another minute. But he had to stay here, aware and on guard. The campground was his to keep safe and the campers were his to watch over.

The ends of the earth. How much farther could he run?

The water in the creek, lapping merrily against its banks, changed the sounds. It made them less identifiable.

He didn't know how long he sat there, the gun lying in his lap, his hands gripping the armrests of the rocking chair. Even when the noise of the fireworks dissipated, he didn't move. The sweat had dried, and his heartbeat had slowed. He could breathe again. But he still didn't move.

Eventually the sound of that breathing became the

only noise he could hear, and he felt irritation that the explosions of fireworks had silenced the night sounds Wil DeWitt called the camper's lullaby.

In the breast pocket of his shirt, Ez's phone vibrated, and he took it out to look at the screen.

—*Sorry if I woke you. 14 down in my puzzle. Middle of a muffin. I am so stuck.*—

Ez hadn't thought he had any smiles left in him tonight, but the text from Joss dug one up. He answered, remembering the clue that had stumped him often enough he thought the word was now forever stamped on his brain, and went into the house.

He put the pistol away in its safe, checking and rechecking its locks, and went back to the kitchen to pour some bourbon. If a time ever came up when he needed to take the edge off, this one qualified. He didn't bother with soda or even ice, just swirled the contents in the bottom of the glass. It was his favorite glass, one he'd found in a cupboard in the old farmhouse and kept. A chip, its indentation smoothed with time, marred its heavy base, but it still fit his hand well.

Everyone had chips, didn't they? Places that were opened by wounds that never really closed properly. Sometimes all you could hope for was a smoothing of the scar. To take the edge off.

He caught sight of his reflection in the wide windows over the kitchen sink. In the dark, wavy image, he looked, in the vernacular he'd grown up with, as if he'd been ridden hard and put away wet. The silver in his hair stood out in bright relief, and the lines that bracketed his mouth were deeper. Even from where he stood, he could see shadows in his eyes where grief and stress haunted them.

The liquid in the glass swirled again, and he couldn't have said whether it was deliberate or if it was because his hands were shaking. He pushed the left one into the pocket of his jeans and looked down at the contents of the glass.

Pressure built behind his eyes. He never cried—a lasting legacy from the old man—but sometimes he wished he could. As it was…

He lifted the glass to his lips and drank. When the bourbon was gone, he shrugged into a jacket and returned to the porch. While the liquor did indeed smooth rough places, it didn't make him sleep. That was just fine with him. Waking dreams were a little easier to control than sleeping ones.

Sometimes… He rubbed a hand over the smooth arm of his chair. Sometimes, he really wished he had a dog.

Chapter Seven

The next day, Joss met June on the porch when she pulled into the driveway behind Joss's car. She would have known her cousin anywhere. She was still elegantly slim, her eyes as blue as Joss's own. Her hair fell into the same soft curve at her shoulders as it had when they were kids, although it was more gray than blond these days. They shared a crushing hug, then stood back to look at each other before hugging again. "You don't have the first wrinkle," Joss accused. "Not to be vain or anything, but my face is starting to fall into accordion pleats. I don't think it's fair."

June laughed, the sound light and silvery. "I always told you guys my clear conscience would pay off someday."

Joss looked toward the small car her cousin had driven. "No Marley today?"

"She wasn't feeling very well and told me to come back tomorrow." June grinned, although concern clouded her eyes. "Of course, she's been telling me that ever since I left home."

They went into the house together. "Go look around," Joss suggested. "I'll make the coffee or pour the wine, whichever's your pleasure."

"A glass first and then a cup. Which room am I in?"

"Just find one with a bed. I'm down here in Gran's

room. You can have that if you want it."

"No, I'd rather use the front one. The boys always got it, remember, because it was the biggest?" June's voice faded as she went up the back stairs. She came back down shortly, her neat slacks and sweater replaced by jeans and a sweatshirt. "If Gray and Seven show up this weekend, it's payback time, isn't it? The only other room with a bed is the back one where you used to sleep."

"I was going to sleep there now, too, until I realized I didn't need to. Gran's room was the first one I got done, so it made sense to sleep there."

They sat across from each other at one end of the long table Joss found in a Prestonsburg estate sale and hauled home in the back of Ez's pickup. She set a half-full bottle of wine and a platter of cheese and crackers between them. The two cousins, three months apart in age, talked and reminisced until both the bottle and the platter were empty, when she replaced one and refilled the other. Darkness fell without them noticing.

Joss looked at the clock. "The last time we were face-to-face was at Gran's funeral, and we didn't get to talk then. Can I ask you now why you became Sister June Esther? I always wondered but was afraid I might go to hell for asking." She grinned at her cousin. "We were dating age at the same time. I don't think being a nun ever came up." June was silent for so long Joss was afraid she'd offended her. "You don't have to answer that if you don't want to. It's not my business."

"Did you know Gran wanted to be a nun?"

"Nothing surprises me about that except that Gran wasn't even Catholic." Joss grinned. "The fact she had a houseful of kids makes me think celibacy might have been a problem, too."

"No, but she wanted to be. She said she thought it was because of Ingrid Bergman in *The Bells of St. Mary's*." June poured the rest of the wine into their glasses and placed more cheese on her plate. "I don't think I'd ever thought that much about it before then, but I liked the idea of a life of service—taking care of Marley had instilled that in me, I guess. Things happened, just like they do in everyone's life, until one day I found myself in Father Paul's office at St. Bridget's asking him how I could enter the religious life."

"What did your folks say?"

June laughed. "They're still saying it. Mother calls from Florida every week saying Dad will rent a trailer, and they'll come and get Marley and me whenever I'm ready, as Dad puts it, to give up the habit for normal clothes. I've never worn a habit, but he thinks if you don't, you're not really a nun."

"That sounds like Uncle Dave. Do you think they'd come up for Thanksgiving? I'd love to make a family reunion of it." To fill Gran's house with the love and laughter she remembered would be such a gift.

"They come up at least once through the holidays, so they probably would. We always tell Marley it's Christmas even if it isn't—she's happy to have more than one. A reunion would be nice, wouldn't it? We haven't all been together since Gran died. What's that been, fifteen years?"

"It was fifteen in August. But I don't even know where Seven is." Joss got up and turned on the coffeemaker.

"Atlantic City. He's part-owner in a casino."

That certainly fit. "Married? Kids? Jail time? You know how Gran worried about him."

"Never on any of the above that I know of. I only know where he is because he donates to our food pantry—almost supports it on his own, to tell the truth. Which I can't, because he's sworn me to secrecy. He keeps up on everyone, though. Did you get something from him when you and Brett divorced?"

Joss couldn't stop the tears that washed over her eyes, but they weren't hot and stinging anymore; rather, they came with tenderness the memory brought forth. "Flowers. A wild, beautiful bunch of them. They smelled like heaven and got me through a few bad days and nights. Will you tell him how much they meant to me? And invite him for Thanksgiving, even if he won't come?"

"I will."

"Do you want to carry our coffee around the campground? We can ride if you'd rather, but walking's really nice."

"I'd love that, although I can't believe you're walking these days." June's eyes sparkled with laughter. "As I recall, you never walked where you could ride."

"That memory's right on the nose." The campground was noisier than usual, with fireworks going off in the distance and music playing well above the decibel level permitted. Joss imagined Ez was walking or riding a golf cart through the campsites looking for the perpetrator.

They stood aside to get out of the way of the hay-filled wagon making its rounds through the property, pulled by two draft horses owned by a farmer from

Colby's Hollow. The farmer was driving the wagon, accompanied by a banjo-strumming Wil DeWitt.

When she saw him, June squealed and waved. "He visits Marley," she explained. "She calls him the big boy who sings."

He nodded, grinning, and raised a hand to wave at them both.

"She talked about him when I was there last, but I never made the connection. She always called Brett the big boy who frowned a lot, something it might have been a good idea for me to pick up on." Joss sighed. When her comment met silence, she turned slowly. "June?"

"I never knew what to say." June's voice was heavy. "I still don't. We had such fun here on the creek as kids. I think we pretended a lot when we were out here, but it didn't protect us from the drama of real life. No matter how much Gran might have wanted to do just that."

"What do you mean?" Joss was afraid she knew what her cousin meant. But even now, when it didn't matter anymore, she didn't want to admit it. She needed for some part of her life to have been what she thought it was.

The music had quieted as they walked, and the fireworks had stopped. Ahead of them on the path, Ez approached from the other direction, looking from side to side. Something inside of Joss warmed and then grew still.

He was starting over, working his way back from places she was absolutely certain had been more difficult than the suspension of her storybook life in Dolan Station. She didn't know what had happened to him—she might never know—but she was certain he'd faced it. "Was it Cassie?" she said into the quiet place between June and herself.

A deep sigh preceded the answer. "She always wanted what you had. In all fairness to her, I don't think she could help it—it's just the way she was. Brett…I don't know, Joss. You knew him better than any of us. You loved him. I think he loved you, too. We just thought you deserved better, that's all."

June's arm came through hers, and it was as if they'd never left the farm.

"I wanted to talk to you about it then, but I was afraid you'd be mad at me and wouldn't believe me."

"You were probably right," Joss admitted. "We were up to our elbows in hormones, and when it came to Brett, I was never the sharpest knife in the drawer anyway." She'd always been aware of the connection between her husband and her sister and had sometimes even been glad for it—he'd been a bridge between Cassie and herself. Until now, she'd denied that the connection had been anything more than a friendship. At the end of her marriage, she hadn't been surprised by his infidelity, but she still hadn't expected the other party to be Cassie.

Wasn't it odd that her sister's betrayal hurt more than her husband's unfaithfulness? It wasn't the first time she'd had the thought, and she hadn't come up with a good answer yet.

June chuckled. "Kind of like Millie with Gray and Uncle Mike with Margaret and me with—" She stopped. "I'm sorry. Did you know the story of your dad and Margaret?"

"She told me after I came here. Lots of odd choices

95

in our family. You and who, by the way, since we're spilling guts here?"

"A kid who lived at the trailer court near Seven. It was all very secretive, because my parents would have lost their minds. He enlisted the summer he graduated and was killed in a training accident. Even now, I'm so sad thinking of him and what a loss that was. At the time, I thought my life ended when his did."

"Is that one of the things that happened that ended with you sitting in Father Paul's office?"

June nodded. "One of them."

Ez was almost abreast with them now. He moved to one side without looking to see who was coming from the other direction.

"Ez." Joss spoke clearly, not raising her voice. She'd learned he didn't respond well to that. "You know my cousin June?"

"We've met." He extended his hand. "Sister."

"Once again, Ezra, June will do. I'm happy to see you again. I'm so pleased with what you've done on Gran and Granddad's farm. I was here before, when the previous owner had it, and I didn't want to come back. The whole place feels different now."

"I'm glad to hear that. Enjoy the weekend. Marley's not with you?"

Disappointment colored his voice, and Joss liked him even better for it.

"Hopefully tomorrow. She wasn't feeling well today."

"I hope so, too." He nodded in the direction from which he'd come. "There's chili and vegetable soup up at the pavilion if you haven't had supper. Margaret made some, and it ended up being a potluck."

Joss had made June's favorite pumpkin spice cake for the weekend. "You ready to share it?"

June sighed. "I am, reluctantly, and chili sounds good. Actually, I brought cornbread with me for Marley—we might as well throw that in the pot, too."

They drove to the pavilion in the UTV, laughing about old days of arguing over who got to drive Granddad's tractor to the mailbox out on the main road and who had to feed Gran's goats. Marley had always gathered the eggs, because the chickens liked her. She called them by name every summer, not realizing many of them weren't the same hens from the year before.

Musicians were tuning up when they parked the utility vehicle and took their offerings to the long table full of food.

While Joss had gotten to know many of the campers and the locals who came to campground events—some of them for the second time, when conversation re-introduced childhood acquaintances— more of them knew June. She'd attracted people that way when they were kids, too. Although Cassie was the one who craved attention, June got it just by being herself. She and Gray referred to themselves as the family showboats, and that's what they were. Cassie resented their popularity, but the rest of the cousins simply enjoyed it.

Joss filled a bowl and took a seat at one of the picnic tables, watching her cousin making her way around the room. Try as she might, she couldn't make herself see Sister June Esther in the pretty woman who laughed with everyone she talked to. "I'll bet she remembers every single person's name," she murmured to no one in particular.

"She does." Ez slid onto the bench beside her, setting a very full bowl of chili down on the table.

"I didn't even know you knew June before today."

His answer was delayed long enough for her to look up. Was it a secret that he and her cousin were acquainted? Or were they more than acquainted? Was that what seemed…off? Was it some of what June didn't want to talk about? The questions whirled through her mind enough that she missed what he said when he spoke. "I'm sorry. What?"

"When I came here, Gray asked me to check on her and Marley. I did, and I guess we became friends of a sort. The texting, phone calls, emails sort. She does puzzles, too. Did you know that?"

"She's the one who got me started on them. We'd sit up in the barn loft on rainy days and do puzzles until Cassie or Marley found us."

He laughed.

She reveled in the sound, thinking how seldom he did that and how nice it was.

"The last hayride of the night leaves the pavilion at ten. Would you like to go on it? You, too." He nodded at June when she sat across the table.

"Not me. It's been a long day, and I'm going to call and check on Marley and then go to bed. I'm looking forward to the rest of the weekend, though." She took a spoonful of chili. "This is so good."

Despite her intentions, June was still there when the hay wagon came around at ten, talking to friends both old and new. She waved Joss on. "You go on ahead. I'll take the cake pan and meet you back at the house." She grinned. "I won't tell Gran if you're late."

Joss sat on a bale of straw on the wagon beside Ez,

breathing in the scent of the night. "I feel like thirty-some years just fell away. Going on a hayride with a cute guy with one of the cousins covering for me with Gran."

He grinned. "I'm not sure I've ever been referred to as a 'cute guy,' at least not that I ever heard."

She leaned away and looked up at him. His smile wrapped itself right around the purely female parts of her, squeezing delightfully. "Take it from me, McIntire," she drawled, "I'm not the first girl who's ever noticed."

The graveled roads through the campground were relatively smooth, although the occasional pothole dug itself. The wagon found one of them, and Joss lurched right into the protective circle of Ez's arm.

"You're welcome, folks." The wagon driver's gleeful chuckle drew answering laughter.

"More and more like high school," Ez murmured, "only a guy was on his own in figuring out how to make his first move."

"Was that a move?" She hoped it was, a thought that startled her. Her breathing quickened and hitched in her chest just exactly as it had when she was a teenager. Apparently some things never changed.

"Yeah." His voice was close to her ear, "I think it was."

****

The wagon stopped at various places on the last trip through the campground to let passengers off near their sites or cabins. Ez jumped off the wagon and helped Joss down before waving the driver on. "I'll walk home. Goodnight, everyone. Thanks for coming to Banjo Creek."

Joss stepped onto the porch and turned to face him. "Do you want a glass of wine or a cup of coffee?"

He shook his head and reached for her hands, standing on the step below her so their faces were nearly level. Her hands were so small in his. Not all that soft—she did too much physical labor—but well cared for. He thought that described her in full; she'd put softness behind her, but she was still taking care of herself. "I wouldn't mind sitting on the porch swing for a little while, though, if you're warm enough."

"I am."

They were so conscious of each other that it was almost laughable. Sitting beside her, her leg beside his, he tried to compose what he wanted to say, which would be a lot easier if he could stop thinking about her leg all warm and straight against his. "If I really were a teenager," he admitted, "I'd be sweating bullets about now. As it is, I'm not real sure of what happens next."

She laughed, the sound hitching a little. "*You'd* be sweating bullets? What about me? I have to worry about my lipstick and about how long it's been since I brushed my teeth."

He grinned back, glad to not be alone in his uncertainty. "You think I don't? Well, not the lipstick, but I haven't shaved in…a while." The addition of scruff to male grooming had been such a gift to people like him. He wondered how Joss felt about scruff.

"I'm attracted to you." He looked straight ahead, not wanting to meet her eyes in the dim glow of the security light on the road. "I won't deny that. Having you at the campground has lightened everything. For the first time since…for the first time in a long time, I feel hopeful." He glanced sidewise at her, feeling sheepish. "That's not a natural state for me. Even before...before things went wrong, I had an innate tendency to always look at the dark side."

She laughed. "I'll bet that endeared you to the girls. We all like dark and mysterious."

"Oh, I wasn't mysterious, just quiet." Although he guessed he'd done all right in the girl department. He hadn't known then what was missing, that his father's dispassion wasn't something to emulate.

Silas had gotten it a long time before he had. Being more open to things had, as Ez warned him, gotten him hurt in the long run. But, in that same long run, Ez had been hurt, too. Shutting himself off hadn't helped at all—not with the old man and not with anything else in life.

"Do you ever wonder if it's all been worth it?" He hadn't meant to ask her that, but the words were there anyway, lying between them.

"No." She lifted a shoulder in a small shrug. "But I have kids. I'm not one of those who thinks you can't have a full life if you're not a parent, but they're the best thing that ever happened in mine."

"But were they enough even when they were home and your whole life?" He felt her warmth in his arm where she brushed against it even through the sweater she wore.

She shook her head. "They were never my whole life—they wouldn't have stood for that for an instant. Even as babies, they weren't cuddlers—if I hadn't been a food source, they wouldn't have missed me. If there was a needy one in the relationship, it was probably me, and I couldn't let them see that. I never wanted them to feel responsible for me—still don't—but I loved being responsible for them. However"—she held up a hand when he started to interrupt—"when they left home, I also loved *not* being responsible for them."

That surprised him. "How did you turn it off?"

"I didn't turn anything off. I don't love them any less, and I'll still be there in a heartbeat if they need me, but the truth is they don't need me anymore—at least not in the all-encompassing parent-child way. I like being busy, but being needed isn't all that important to me." Her grin had a cynical edge. "It was one of the revelations that came with being single not-by-choice."

"I've never thought about being needed, maybe because I don't have kids, but I still feel responsible for…too many things, I guess." No guessing to it—he knew he did. But he didn't know how *not* to bear that weight. No amount of counseling or bourbon-born wisdom had taught him that.

"You need to answer your own question." Her voice fell quiet into the darkness. "Do you wonder if it's all been worth it?"

"Every single day." The words burst forth, as if they'd been waiting for a long time to be said. The alarm came and went on her face so quickly he wasn't sure he'd seen it, but her hand taking his and holding on hard told him it had been real.

"Not…I don't think about suicide." That wasn't true. He thought about it frequently, but not with any intent in mind. "There was sniper fire in Iraq—" Nothing like jumping into the middle of the story. "I should have been prepared. It was my team, my responsibility to keep them safe. I didn't do it. Two people died." He had to push the words out, snapping them off like pieces of hard plastic.

He still woke in the middle of the night seeing their faces. No one had blamed him—even the team members' wives hadn't. They'd offered him more comfort at their husbands' funerals than he'd deserved.

It should have been him. He was the pilot. It was his team.

It should have been him.

"Please."

Just the one word, spoken softly beside him, gave pause to the siege of his thoughts. He turned just enough to see her face and catch a glimpse of shimmer in her eyes.

"I value you." Her voice was quiet. Gentle and firm at the same time. "All the people here do. You give them a safe place, and sometimes, like when we're gathered up at the pavilion, you're an instrument of hope for some of them. You need to value yourself, Ezra McIntire."

Before he could look away, she lifted her hands…small, warm, and capable…to frame his face. Her eyes–still damp, still shimmering–held his gaze for a moment before they drifted closed, and her lips touched his. Timorously at first, as if she were doing something she hadn't in a long time, and then deeper. Warmer.

Ez didn't know, as she pulled away and he drew her in for more, if knowing her…holding her…would allow him to value himself. But he did understand, from that first suggestion of a kiss, that he valued her, and that these moments shared on the porch of the old farmhouse were the best ones he'd had in more time than he could remember. Value. Yes, value.

Chapter Eight

Joss showered, got ready for bed, and sat in Gran's rocker beside the kitchen fireplace to write in her journal. *I feel like a sixteen-year-old girl recovering from a broken heart. Tonight I kissed a man for the first time since Brett, and guess what—I'm alive. I'm alive!*

"Hey, cuz, you still up?"

She hadn't heard June come down the back stairs. "Hot chocolate?" she asked, glad not to be alone. That surprised her—she'd spent enough of the past months without company that she'd learned to like solitude much more than she'd expected.

"I'll make it." June went to the refrigerator. "You're doing wonders with the house. It feels as if Gran is still here, only with a dishwasher, a self-cleaning oven, and a clothes dryer that works."

When the chocolate was ready, the women sat across from each other at the table as they had earlier in the day. "He's handsome." June licked a creamy moustache off her top lip.

"Who?"

The blue eyes that were a mirror of her own gazed skyward for a few beats, then June snorted.

"That's not very attractive, a snorting nun." But then they were both laughing. Choking and coughing, they yanked paper napkins out of the basket on the table and blew their noses.

"The guy"—June wiped her streaming eyes—"you were spooning on the porch swing with."

"Spooning?" Joss was off again. "Did you hear that, Gran?" It was her turn to look up. "June thinks I was *spooning*. I'm sure neither of us has heard that word since we last heard it from you or Granddad."

"I've been living in a protected environment," June said righteously. "Spooning is a perfectly correct term—"

"It is not. It wasn't even thirty-some years ago when we really were doing…that on the front porch. Which we weren't. Ez and me, I mean. We weren't." Heat rose in Joss's cheeks. She couldn't take credit for the *spooning* not having gone further than a few kisses. Several kisses. And a long, warm embrace before he left.

"Hmm…okay." June, still smirking, reached for the notebook and pen lying beside the napkin basket. "Since we're still awake, and one of us is blushing, let's make a list of the people you want to invite to Thanksgiving. You sure you want to invite my folks? My dad will be all over me about the nun business."

"That's Uncle Dave." Joss would so love to see the uncle who wanted to fix all their lives whether they needed it or not. "If he's all over you, he's not picking on anyone else. It's your duty to take on that responsibility. Besides, if they're here, Aunt Eileen will make the dressing. I won't have to embarrass myself. She uses Gran's recipe."

"Yeah, and unlike the rest of us, Mom does it right." June wrote her parents' names at the top of the list, then added Gray's parents, Gray, and Seven. "Your kids?"

"Yes, but they won't be able to come." She couldn't think about not seeing them for the holiday. Although she was mostly accustomed to not seeing them as often as she'd like, there were times… "Any of your friends?"

"I'll ask. Romy? You and she seem to have gotten close. And Margaret?"

"Yes. And Wilson, too." She leaned an elbow on the table, propping her chin on her palm. "I think they're an item."

"What about the guy? The spooning one?"

God would take June in hand—she wasn't acting very nun-like. "Him, too."

"Do you want to invite your mother?"

Joss leaned back in her chair, tugging her worn chenille robe closer around her body to ward against the sudden chill. The idea of *not* inviting her mother felt wrong, but having her here would undoubtedly feel more so. "I'm sure she'll be with Cassie and Brett." Her eyes widened with a sudden horrifying thought. "Should I invite them, too? Cassie's still a cousin." She chewed on the end of her thumbnail. "What if I invite them and they come?"

June didn't answer, just sat quietly, doodling beside the list she'd started. After a few minutes and several drawings of kittens, she said quietly, "What if? It's the closest thing to a level playing field you'll ever find, yet the fact that you've done all the work to make this place as wonderful as it once was gives you—since I'm talking sports here—home court advantage. If they come, they're going to know that." She pointed her pen at Joss. "And if they show up and you offer to let them have Gran's room, I'll smack you."

She looked so much like the June of summers past that Joss had to blink back tears. She got up. "More hot chocolate?"

"Sure. I've already had a week's worth of liquid today—what's another pint or so?"

June's voice followed her.

"You know, the fanciest thing I wear is a bra with lace I got from the clearance rack, but I wouldn't be caught dead in that robe."

"Sure, you would." Joss laughed, doing a little twirl. "It was Gran's. I found it in a trunk in the attic. You know her—she wouldn't get rid of anything as long as there were still two threads connected. It was in there with her wedding dress and some other things. I left the rest alone until the rest of you could choose from it, but I absconded with the robe."

She poured their chocolate and resumed her seat. "Go ahead and write Mother and Cassie and Brett down. I'll send the invitations and the numbers of all the motels in a twenty-mile radius. If they come, they're for sure not going to camp. The cabins aren't fancy enough, and the bedrooms in the house are already reserved."

June propped her chin in her palm. "At the risk of crossing a line of privacy between cousins, what bothers you the most about seeing Cassie and Brett? Is it the idea of seeing them together?"

"No. That part, at least, is past." Joss captured a floating island of whipped cream on her tongue and took her time swallowing it. "But there are two truths even with that out of the way. First off, I miss Cassie. It seems crazy even to me, but I do. This is the first time we've ever gone this long without communicating.

Even when we argued more than we talked, it was still contact. Yet I'm not ready to be close to her. I may never be."

"I can understand that." June drew a spotted puppy in the margin of the notebook. "What's the other truth?"

"It's embarrassing." Joss sipped her chocolate, frowning. "I'm afraid to see Brett, in case I still have feelings for him. I don't think I do, but I loved him for over half my life. I don't know if that's all gone or not."

"It's natural, I think, to still feel something for someone you spent that long with," June observed, "but don't confuse that feeling for being in love. I know." She held up a hand. "I know being a nun doesn't qualify me to make any kind of a statement about that, but lots of the people I spend time with are ones who are in your shoes, whose lives jumped up and kicked them in the butt when they weren't looking. They always say they know they need to face down what hurt them, but they don't. Neither do you." She picked up the pen. "I can scratch out their names just as easily as I wrote them."

Joss looked at the names on the list, written in June's artistic hand. No matter what had gone before, Brett was still the boys' father. Cassie was still their aunt and her sister. Ignoring the relationship because she didn't like it anymore would be like painting the walls white to avoid things clashing.

Not happening. No white walls for this Murphy cousin. "Leave them. If they don't come, they're the ones missing a good time."

"Right." June beamed. "And now, dear cousin, I'm going to bed. We nuns, righteous souls that we are, need our sleep." She rose and came around the table to hug Joss. "I'm so glad to have this time together."

"Me, too. Sleep tight, Sister Cousin. See you in the morning."

When June had gone up the back stairs, Joss returned to the front porch. Although the hour was late, she was tired, but not sleepy. She'd had a wonderful day. She wanted to take her time and remember its parts. Spending time with June, the evening at the pavilion…

Kissing Ezra McIntire.

Excitement rose in her chest again, making her heart do funny things. She smiled into the night, then got up and went into her room to replace Gran's robe with a jacket and snag a flashlight from the closet. She was too edgy to go to bed, too happy to sleep if she did.

Happy. Yes. And the feeling was all kinds of wonderful.

****

He hadn't kissed a woman since Lucy.

He hadn't felt like this since…man, maybe never.

The campground was quiet. Lights were still on both inside and outside some trailers and motor homes, and people in lawn chairs surrounded the occasional campfire. No music broke the natural hum of night sounds.

The autumn night was perfect. Cool enough to qualify as crisp, but as long as you had on a sweatshirt, it was still a good time to be outside.

He drove a golf cart instead of the UTV in deference to the stillness, but on the basketball court, two teenagers played Horse. The *whomp-whomp-whomp* of the ball was somehow not discordant. He and Silas used to sneak out of the house after the old man was asleep and shoot hoops in the empty barn on a farm a mile away. The Barnett boys and Pete Hilliard would come, too. They never got caught. Only in long retrospect did he realize they hadn't gotten caught because everyone's parents probably knew where they were.

He'd intended to go home and go to bed after leaving Joss on her porch earlier in the evening, but settling in escaped him. He couldn't turn off his mind.

Could he have a relationship? Did he have it in him? Or, if he tried, would he hurt both Joss and himself? PTSD was hard on everyone, not just the one who suffered from it. What would she do if he had a flashback, or even if he cowered in place because he couldn't be certain he was hearing fireworks instead of mortar fire? She'd been hurt enough by betrayal. How could he ask her to take a chance on being hurt by another man, even if it was in an entirely different way?

He drove around the building that housed the office and the camp store, stopping to make sure the doors were locked, then drove to the restaurant building. The locks and alarm were secure.

Very few campers were on the road, although a few couples rode bicycles toward Colby's Hollow, and some walkers sauntered from the direction of the creek. Only one walked alone, and he pulled up beside her. "Want a ride?"

Joss smiled at him. "Where you headed, mister?"

"Nowhere in particular. You?"

She came around and climbed into the golf cart beside him. "Me, either. I was just restless."

He chuckled. "I know the feeling."

They rode in silence for a few minutes, then spoke

at the same time.

"What are you—"

"Will you join us for Thanksgiving?"

"I'd like that." He didn't know if he would or not, but he liked having been asked. He hoped— "Will Gray be here?"

"I don't know. I'm asking him. I haven't seen him in years."

"Me, either. Not in person, anyway." He'd like nothing better than to see Grayson Douglas. Maybe if he talked to someone who understood how things had been then, he could find some peace. It was a long shot. But maybe. "Why don't you concentrate on the house until then?" he suggested. "Have it as ready for vacation rental status as can be achieved. It'll be comfortable for your gathering."

"You're sure you wouldn't mind if I did that? You're still the boss, and I'm nowhere near done painting in the cabins."

"It'll be good for the campground to have it done."

"I'll need to find a place to live once you're able to list it as a rental."

He hadn't thought of that. He wished he had, because the truth was, he didn't want her to leave the campground. "You can move back into Cabin Three. At least until spring."

She nodded, hesitancy in the gesture. "If that works out, I'll do that. Eventually, though, I'll want…" She stopped. "I don't know. Something more permanent."

"With no white walls."

"Right."

They rode around the campground one more time, talking about the differences between growing up in suburban Nashville and rural Missouri.

"I'll bet you were on the homecoming court," he said. "Maybe not a cheerleader, though."

"Neither. I worked in the library in both high school and college."

"Is library science your degree?"

"No degree. I only went for a year, then quit and got married. And I studied interior design. In retrospect, I have no idea why. I like color a lot, and I'm glad to know how to use it, but working in the library was what satisfied me."

"Was it something your parents wanted you to do?"

She chewed a thumbnail, her expression thoughtful. "I got my love of color from my dad—he painted watercolors. My mother has an incredible eye for design. I expect I thought I could please her and make myself happy at the same time." She shrugged. "Not a particularly smart move on my part. What about you?"

"I went to college right out of high school, but it didn't work out, so I enlisted after my second year and took classes and got my bachelor's and master's degrees while I was active. After Iraq—" He stopped. What was he doing? This wasn't something he talked about, but he couldn't just ignore her questioning look. "I retired," he said. "Got my doctorate and taught at the college level. I was lucky. I loved flying helicopters, and I loved teaching."

"But you don't do either anymore?"

The question scraped a raw place he tried to keep covered. Enough time had passed since his retirement that much of military life seemed like a dream. He seldom thought about flying a chopper, although he missed being in the air. But the classroom and the drive-him-crazy students within it—he thought he'd miss them every day of his life.

He liked the campground. He liked not having the paralyzing worry about his contingent of students. But he missed teaching, missed watching them learn. Working in education was such a *good* way to be driven crazy. He'd love to go back.

The thought made him laugh, a silent chuckle he couldn't explain to Joss, although he wanted to. He thought she'd understand. "No," he said, "I don't." And then the surprise came. "Maybe someday."

****

Marley looked, as Gran would have said, peaked. She was still as beautiful as she'd always been, but her appearance had a waiflike quality that hadn't used to be there. Joss had seen her three times since coming to Banjo Bend, and she seemed to fade a little each time. "Is it her heart?" She was on the porch with June, watching Marley handing candy to trick-or-treaters, her delighted laughter floating up to where they sat.

June nodded. "We always knew it would fail eventually, and it seems to be doing just that. She doesn't really understand, other than she's tired. She'll always feel better *tomorrow*. I used to wish she was different than she is, but I've learned better in these years of looking after her. We should all be so happy, and we should all share it like she does."

Joss didn't want to think of a world without Marley in it sharing butterflies and rainbows with everyone she thought needed them. "Do your folks know it's happening?"

"They're in denial, I think. They'll know when they come to visit. Mom's going to want to take her back to Florida with them." June closed her eyes, and the hand resting on the arm of her chair fisted. "It will take some talking to convince her otherwise."

"You're her guardian, aren't you?"

"Legally, yes." June waited a beat. "I don't know what's going to happen with her health, but I don't want her to be afraid. She loves where she lives, and her roommates are as much her family as we are. I won't have her uprooted from everything she knows."

"I'm glad."

Trick-or-treating ended almost right to the minute at nine o'clock. They left the porch. "Ready to go in, Marley?" June asked. "Have you had fun?"

"I still have candy." Marley peered past her sister in search of more strangely dressed visitors. "Here comes that big boy."

Joss waved at the hay wagon as it approached.

Ez jumped down and approached where Marley sat with her orange plastic bucket of treats. He waved at Joss and June, but his attention was for Marley. "Trick or treat." He smiled down at her.

She handed him a candy bar.

He put it into the pocket of his denim shirt and knelt in front her chair. "Want a ride?"

Her eyes widened, and she pointed at the wagon. "Up there?"

"Yep."

"Can I, June?"

June nodded, moving forward to help her out of her chair.

"Seems to me"—Wyatt Iverson spoke from the

114

driver's seat of the wagon—"it's time for Miss Marley to learn to drive these horses. Would you like that?"

She nodded so enthusiastically it made Joss's head ache. She stepped forward to help get her cousin into the seat beside the pastor, then moved back so June could climb up beside her. "You two have fun."

Ez came to stand beside Joss.

They waved the wagon off. "How's it gone today?" she asked. The only part she'd taken in the Halloween activities that day was driving Marley around in the UTV.

"Fine, I think. The kids have had fun, at least."

"Coffee?"

"Only if I can have it to go. The music's starting at the pavilion. You want to take me up there in the UTV? The hay wagon will stop there and let June and Marley off."

"Sure. Are you playing?"

"Not tonight." He pushed back the baseball cap that semi-controlled his hair. "I thought maybe you'd be my date."

His date. There would be no denying the word now. He'd said it. She'd managed to convince herself they were friends, and they were. Several dinners together, long conversations as they walked the campground roads, and silent, strong-shouldered support when they each recognized the other having a bad day had cemented that relationship. But it was more than that.

She didn't kiss the rest of her friends on the front porch and think about the contact far into the night and the next day. She was always glad to see them, but none of them made her heart leap…and keep beating fast well beyond the time that was even reasonable.

What if…what if the question she'd raised with June wasn't just a manifestation of her need to have something to worry about? If she still had feelings for Brett, it meant she wasn't ready for dating, didn't it?

She smiled at Ez, thinking he did a lot for a baseball cap. She thought he might do a lot for anything he chose to wear, although she'd never seen him in anything but jeans and a flannel shirt or the same jeans and a sweatshirt. He wore the jeans very well. "You bet, McIntire," she said. "I'll be your date."

Chapter Nine

"You're afraid of heights." Ez stood between Joss and the stepladder on Wednesday morning after the Halloween weekend, hands on his hips. "You've painted half the ceilings in the entire campground, including the ones in this house, and never thought to mention that fact? How have you done it? More to the point, *why* have you done it?"

"It's what you hired me for, remember? I've been afraid of heights my whole life, and I've been painting ceilings for most of it. Now, if you want me to climb up on the roof, we might have a problem. I could climb up, but I couldn't get down, whereas the stepladder in here and I have an agreement. If I can't reach the ceiling from the third step, I call someone." She gestured toward the back staircase. "I can't do that. I can paint everywhere I can reach, but I don't do scaffolds." She sidestepped neatly, getting to the ladder and its first step. "How did you find out I was afraid of heights, anyway?"

"You knew 'acrophobe' right away on yesterday's crossword."

"It's not exactly difficult." She rolled her eyes. "Not on par with 'vowellike.' I still don't think that's a real word." She knew it was, but she was still irritated that he'd gotten it, and she hadn't.

"It's not a usual one, either." He looked toward the

clock on the wall. "I came to ask a favor. If you'll make a run to Lexington for me, I'll finish this ceiling and take care of the high stuff in the staircase."

She stifled a sigh. She didn't mind the trip to Lexington, but it seemed as if Ez always wanted her to go somewhere when she was in the middle of something else. She could count on one hand the times she knew he'd physically left the campground since she'd come two months before.

"Margaret has a doctor's appointment, all very secretive, and she's bound and determined she's going to drive herself," he explained. "I don't normally have a problem with that, but she's upset about something. I thought maybe you could say you had to pick up something for me. You can take the truck."

"I'll take my car, and we'll go to dinner before we head back." They might go shopping, too, if Margaret was up to it. Joss had very few clothes to go into winter with, and none of them fit. She liked that—she'd gained fifteen pounds post-divorce that her small frame hadn't accommodated very well. Losing that had made her feel more like herself.

Additionally, no matter how much she liked painting, she didn't like ceilings, so she wasn't all that sorry to turn that part of the job over to Ez. "What time is Margaret's appointment?"

He looked at the clock on the microwave. "Two."

Joss followed his gaze and stepped down from the ladder, handing him her roller. "In that case, here you go. I have time to change my clothes and brush my teeth. Does she know one of us is taking her?"

"Yeah. She's over at the office fuming about it. Wil's taking her place in there today, and she's telling him how to do everything just like he hadn't spent almost as much time here as she has."

Joss hurried back to her room to change clothes. She put on lipstick and mascara and twisted her hair into a messy bun, then returned to the kitchen.

Ez turned to look at her. "You look nice."

She poured coffee into two commuter cups and prepared the pot again, not meeting his bemused expression. Her cheeks heated more with every move she made. What was it about being told she looked nice that should make her blush? "Thank you. The coffeepot is ready whenever you want some. Just push the button. Text me if you need us to pick anything up in Lexington."

When he smiled, she thought she might just melt where she stood. A blush, weak knees, and remembering to put on mascara when it wasn't even Sunday—what was she coming to?

"Okay. You two be careful."

Margaret came out to the car when Joss stopped in front of the office.

"This is ridiculous." She settled into the passenger seat with a huff. "I've been driving myself for over fifty years and suddenly I need a caretaker?" She yanked her seatbelt into place and glared at the windshield.

"I don't know. Do you?" Joss tapped the top of one of the cups between them. "This one's yours. Are you going to be grumpy all the way to Lexington?"

"No, I don't, and no, I'm not." Margaret picked up her cup. "Thank you for the coffee."

"So, do you want to tell me why you're going to a doctor two hours away?"

"I had breast cancer ten years ago and have to get

scans every year. I feel fine, but the scans always make me a little jumpy. Maybe a lot jumpy." Margaret sipped, closing her eyes with a grateful little purr. "Let's not talk about me. I'm not interesting."

"Sure, you are." Joss turned onto the road that led through Banjo Bend to the highway. "Wilson thinks you are, for sure." Margaret's blush made her feel better about her own less than a half hour before. Maybe it was just something in the coffee.

"Wil's a dear heart," said Margaret. "He reminds me of your dad. Into music instead of painting, but still very artistic. Funny, but never at anyone else's expense."

"That does sound like Dad." Joss smiled at her passenger. "Sounds like he makes you happy. Is that like Dad, too?"

"In a way, yes, it is. And it's better, because Wil and I kind of know what to do with how we feel about each other in a way your dad and I never did." Margaret chuckled. "There are good things about being old, and being surer of yourself in relationships is one of them. Or maybe you care less—I'm not sure which. Either way, it's more comfortable than being in love at seventeen or even in your twenties."

"What about in your forties?" Joss hadn't meant to ask the question, but since she had, she was anxious to hear its answer. She knew—now—that although she'd always loved Brett, she hadn't been *in* love with him for years. She also knew he'd once loved her, but passing time made her wonder if he'd ever been *in* love with her. Or had it always been Cassie who'd filled his heart when he was alone?

"I can't give you answers on that, although we both

know I like to think I know everything. My husband was still living then, and we had a good life together. We loved each other. In retrospect—" She stopped, looking out the side window. A tear slid down her cheek. "I probably shouldn't have married him, although I'm not sorry I did, and I don't think he was ever sorry, either."

"Because of Dad?"

"Yes. Not that I didn't know that was over. He'd married your mother, so of course I knew it. But I was still carrying a big, bright-lit torch for him when Danny and I eloped to Vegas."

"I wish he'd married you." Joss wasn't going to say she wished Margaret had been her mother, although she suspected it might be true. "I think he'd have been happier."

"That's a nice thing to say, honey." Margaret patted her hand on the steering wheel. "But he loved your mother, I think, and I know he loved you girls. I saw him at the end of one summer when he came to pick you up. I was in Banjo Bend to visit family. We had a drink and took a walk together." Margaret's voice thinned and wobbled. "I never told anyone before about that day."

"You still loved each other, didn't you?" *Like Cassie and Brett.* The thought wasn't painful—at least, not really—more melancholy than anything.

"No." Margaret's answer was instant. "Love's not static." She hesitated, turning her face back toward the side window again. "At least, I don't think it is, and when Mike and I let it go, it never had a chance to grow. I suppose, if I'm honest about it, I wish things had been different, but they weren't. Period."

"I shouldn't have married Brett, either." Joss turned onto the highway and reached for her cup. "More to that point, I guess, Brett shouldn't have married me. There's a difference, isn't there?"

"There is."

They rode in companionable silence for a while. Margaret took a drink of coffee, then turned sideways, yanking at her seatbelt to give her room. "You and the boss seem to be getting along really well. He hardly ever says any more than necessary, but you seem to have found the conversational side to him."

"We talk about the campground and paint colors." And music and crossword puzzles and books. They discussed and compared how they'd grown up, whose chili was better, and when and whether the music really had died when Buddy Holly, Richie Valens, and the Big Bopper did.

They never talked about kissing…or what kisses meant. But since that first time on the porch a few nights ago, they'd found several opportunities to explore the subject further. They didn't talk about dating, either, but Joss thought it was very possible that's exactly what they were doing. Maybe. Probably.

She needed to think about something else. "Was there anyone you wanted me to invite to Thanksgiving? Wil's coming, but if you have family you'd like to have, we can ask them."

"Thank you, but there's no one." For just an instant, the twinkle left Margaret's gray-blue eyes. "The campground's kind of my family." She gave her head a little shake. "How are you coming with the menu? What should I bring? I'm a whiz with homemade dinner rolls."

"Say no more. That will be perfect. If my kids could come—which they can't—you'd have to double the batch."

"I'll bet you miss them."

"I do, but it's been seven years since they've lived at home. Even during summers while they were in college, they were working somewhere else. That's how they ended up in Oregon."

"What are you going to do when they have children?"

Joss laughed. "Buy more plane tickets."

The afternoon passed quickly. After Margaret's scans, they spent a couple of hours in a mall before having dinner.

"Does this make you miss the city?" Margaret frowned at the menu. "There's so much more to do. So many more choices."

Joss nodded, looking around the dining room that managed to be both large and intimate at the same time. "It's fun to come here, and I admit living so far out in the country takes some getting used to, but there isn't really much I miss. I don't know how I'll feel at the end of the time I've allowed myself to decide what I want to do, but for now, I'm content at the campground."

And anxious to get back, she acknowledged when they left the restaurant. If she didn't watch herself, she was going to end up as reclusive as Ez. The thought made her chuckle, and Margaret gave her a curious look.

"I always had something to do, somewhere to go, people to be with," Joss explained. "I liked all of it— my job, my friends, my community. I was mad at Brett for a lot of things, but I think that was the biggest. He didn't just ruin the marriage—he ruined my way of life. Does that mean I'm shallow?"

Margaret laughed. "If it does, there's a lot of it going around. I don't know if it's a gender thing or what, but everyone I know examines her life and the motives within it the same way. I did, too—that's why I know I shouldn't have married Danny. But hindsight…you know…it's twenty-twenty and all that. The thing to do is learn from it and go on."

"I agree, but what if I'm directionally challenged? What if I 'go on' the wrong way?"

"Then you turn around."

"Okay." A minute later, Joss snorted laughter. "It's a good thing you told me the right thing to do, because I just missed my exit."

****

Banjo Creek had a downright blissful autumn weather-wise, but it seemed Mother Nature read calendars. November brought with it frosty mornings, sluggish heating systems, and—in the middle of the night after Joss and Margaret had gone to Lexington— six inches of heavy, wet snow.

Ez, cruising the campground road the following Tuesday with the snowblade on the front of the tractor, didn't think a lot of it—Missouri had offered this treat several times in early November when he was a kid. He was just happy he didn't have cows to milk these days.

No one else at the campground seemed happy at all. Only a few of them remained after the college kids and interns were gone for the season, but grumpiness could fill a room pretty quickly. Margaret and Wilson were at the office taking inventory in the store and cleaning the storeroom. A few minutes with them made

Ez relieved to fill his commuter cup and get back on the tractor. The job was cold, but at least no one out there was mad at anybody.

When he got to the farmhouse, Joss was shoveling her sidewalk. He wanted to take the shovel from her—the thing was dang near as big as she was—but he was pretty sure she wouldn't thank him for it. He swung down from the tractor and approached her. "How much trouble would I be in if I—"

"Don't find out." She straightened with a decidedly unkind look. "I like this almost as much as painting ceilings, but I do need to be able to take care of myself. Besides, I'm nearly done. Then I'm going to Romy's and eating a double order of biscuits and gravy."

He'd had Romy's biscuits and gravy. He'd love to have them again. "You want to bring me back an order?" he asked. "I'd go, but—"

"No, you wouldn't." She pushed snow off the last few feet of her path and straightened again, twisting from side to side. "You never want to leave the campground. If you don't have a reason to stay here, you think one up."

He opened his mouth to argue the point, then closed it again. She was right.

"It's okay." She leaned the shovel against the picket fence that surrounded the house. "It's your choice if you want to stay here and your business why, but don't make excuses. Not to me." She turned toward her house, then back around again. "Did you want something?"

"What?"

"When you stopped, did you want something?"

Her cheeks were rosy from effort, her hair

tumbling loose from her hat. Her eyes sparkled—they always sparkled—but they held a different expression than usual. Something like hurt. He didn't want to be the cause of that. "Actually." He cleared his throat. "I just stopped to help you shovel. Now that I'm here" — he cleared it again— "maybe you'd let me take you to breakfast at Romy's. I'll buy."

Her eyes widened. He'd read somewhere about a guy getting lost in a woman's eyes and snickered at the very idea. He wasn't snickering now; instead, he was as lost as anyone had ever been. *Keep it simple, stupid. Don't get serious.* "But if you're having a double order, we may have to revisit that."

"Oh, well."

She seemed flustered, which delighted him much more than it should have. If he hadn't been a guy, he would have giggled.

"I guess I can make do with a single order. And coffee. Lots of coffee."

"Absolutely." He nodded. "I'll park this and get my truck and be back in about twenty minutes, if that's all right."

She nodded, too. Twice. Briskly. "I'll be ready."

He might have pushed the tractor a little hard on the way to his house, considering its age and how hard he'd already worked it that morning, but the *Old Girl* performed admirably. She earned the name painted on her hood. He probably only imagined he heard her breathe a sigh of relief when he pulled into the equipment shed. He gave the hood a pat when he walked past.

After a two-minute shower, he put on his newest jeans and the flannel shirt Margaret gave him for his

126

birthday. The red-and-black plaid was a lot nicer than the ones he bought himself. He gave thought to shaving but decided against it.

When he pulled up in front of the farmhouse, Joss was already on its freshly shoveled path. She was wearing black jeans and a white puffy coat he'd never seen before, a colorful scarf hanging down its front. Her hair was in the messy bun he liked best, and she was wearing makeup. Not that he noticed things like that. At least, not usually.

Romy's was packed, of course. He suppressed a groan. Eating in a public restaurant was one thing, that half of Banjo Bend was in the same place was quite another. Most of the diners came to the pavilion on music nights, but still, the crowded room made his heart pump hard. While they waited for a booth to empty, he looked around. He knew half the guys in there and some of the women carried guns, and he didn't care. Honestly, he didn't. But the knowledge made the hair on the back of his neck stand up, and he wanted to rub his spine on the doorjamb to ease the prickles there.

Romy waved from the back, leaned over to clean a table, and pointed down at it.

Oh, good, he'd be able to sit facing out at the room. Unless Joss wanted to. Maybe they could share one side of the booth. What if she wanted to look out at the rest of the diners? She was a people watcher—they'd talked about that. He'd laughed at her when she'd told him airports were some of her favorite places. He wasn't sure he could stay there if he had to have his back to the room.

But she slid into the side with her back to the others, and he wondered if she'd known. They'd talked a lot; she knew he had a little PTSD problem—although not its scope. Maybe she'd just understood. Either way, by the time he'd taken the seat across from her and turned his cup upright to be filled, his heartbeat had slowed to normal and his back and neck felt like themselves again. He reached up to smooth the hair on his nape, though, in case it really was standing out the way it had felt like it was.

"So good to see you both!" Romy filled their cups, laid down menus, and gave Joss a one-armed hug. "Joss, I know you want biscuits and gravy with hash browns. Do you know what you'd like, Ez, or do you want to check out the menu?"

"Hi, Romy." He returned her smile, which was easier than he'd expected. He liked her. "I'll just take what the painter lady's having." When Romy left to place their orders, he directed his attention to Joss. "What's next on your agenda at the campground? The house is about done, right? At least, for the time being. I imagine if it's successful, we'll add on to it. A couple more bedrooms and another bath, at least. You're good on appliances?"

"Good on everything since the mattresses are ordered. You'll want bedsteads, too, but I didn't know what you'd want to do about that."

He reacted every time the door opened, looking up even if she was talking, which annoyed him considerably. He needed to concentrate on what she was saying, not on the rush of air that accompanied every arrival to the café. "I've trusted you so far. You've spent far less than I would have and gotten much better results. I'm not going to start doubting you now. What do you want to do?"

"Vintage. There are enough thrift shops and antiques stores between here and Prestonsburg, I shouldn't have any trouble."

"Sounds good. You'll be ready for your Thanksgiving extravaganza then?"

She laughed. "Not a word that fits the Murphy cousins, I don't think. But, yes, I'll be ready and so will the house. I already heard from Gray. He'll be here. He was going to get reservations at a motel rather than take one of the bedrooms in the farmhouse. I think he's afraid he'll end up having to share a bathroom with the girl cousins again."

"He can stay with me if you don't have enough space." Ez hadn't meant to offer; he didn't have much faith in his own in-house hospitality. But it was Gray, after all. He looked forward to seeing him.

Their breakfast came momentarily, and for a while they were too busy eating to talk. "I was thinking about the week between Christmas and New Year's. Are you going to open the campground for it?" Joss set down her cup.

"Yes. Not the tent sites, but cabins, campers, and motor homes. We already have some reservations."

"You could rent the house, too, to a large family."

He couldn't deny that renting the house would pump welcome funds into the business, but— "You're still living in it, Joss."

"But I don't have to. You could rent the house out all winter, Ez. It would be good money."

"What do you mean, you don't have to? You don't want to winter in a cabin. I know we agreed to it, but moving out of the house every time someone rented it will grow old fast, too—like the first time you have to do it." He had to swallow panic. If she didn't live at the campground, she'd move back to Tennessee. Or, worse yet, out west to live close to her kids. He'd never see her again, unless the Murphy cousins rented their grandparents' house for a reunion weekend.

"I'm not sure yet what I'll do." Joss smiled thanks at the waitress who refilled their cups on her way past. "But I do know I'm not going to be a burden to anyone. If I stay in a house that you can reasonably expect to keep rented nearly all the time, that's exactly what I'll be."

"You wouldn't." But he understood, reluctantly, because he'd have felt the same way in her shoes. "You'll let me know once you decide?"

"Yes."

He had the feeling she wanted him to say more, but he didn't know what. Or how. All he knew for sure was that she was probably going to leave, and he could stand to think about it.

Chapter Ten

She'd wanted him to ask her to stay. Obviously, she'd put more personal stock into their "seeing each other" than he had. It had been such fun, going out for breakfast and talking all through it. He'd even shared conversation with others who had stopped by their table. His enthusiasm about improvements to the house and other areas of the campground was infectious.

But then the conversation had turned to the fact that she was living in the house. He'd said she didn't have to leave, and Joss was sure he'd meant it. But he didn't offer much in the way of alternatives, either.

The bad part, the really bad part, was that Joss didn't even know what she wanted. She'd only been at the Creek for a couple of months—nowhere near the six she'd allotted herself to make a decision, but she should be closer to knowing…knowing where she would spend Act Two. Of her life, that was. Because that's what this was.

Making life choices without having to consider the wishes of parents or a husband or even her kids was exciting in a way, but she wasn't the living-out-of-a-suitcase type. She wanted to have her own "stuff" again. Not the things she'd left behind in Dolan Station—they were a part of Act One that she'd left behind the curtain permanently—but belongings for Act Two. She'd taken her maiden name back in the divorce, and she wanted to *be* Joss Murphy again.

However, being Joss Murphy meant having a significant interest in Ezra McIntire, and that didn't seem to be working out very well.

She finished painting in the house that day. Although much of the outside trim needed paint or repair or both, that would have to wait until spring. Painting the porch had given the house a much-needed facelift. Thanks to Ez lending her the labor of the college kids, the landscaping was neat and ready for any season.

She and Margaret had spent an entire afternoon ordering hospitality items online. As soon as Ez decided how much to charge and upped his insurance, the house was ready to list on vacation rental sites.

And ready for her to move out of. It was like summer's end in the years of spending July and August with her grandparents. She'd ridden, silent and morose in the backseat of her parents' car, back to Nashville. Back to the everything-in-its-place bedroom that was hers but never really hers. Her mother always redid the girls' rooms in the summer, so they suited her taste instead of theirs. The changes had worked for Cassie—not so much for Joss.

Ez would undoubtedly let her remain in one of the cabins. They were rented only part of the time through the winter. But Joss, Act Two, wanted a house no one could make her leave. She didn't have to own it—at least not until after the six months were up and she'd decided where the stage would be for this act—but she did want to hang pictures and curtains and make sure there weren't any white walls while she was there.

She showered and dressed again. She'd been going

to stay in and read, but she was restless. The snow hadn't melted, but there hadn't been wind in it to create drifts, so driving wasn't a problem. She wanted to go…somewhere.

In answer to the thought, her phone rang.

"It's taco Tuesday at Corporal's, and I have the night off. Want to go?" Romy sounded cheerful and expectant.

"I'd love it. Where and what is Corporal's?"

"It's the bar and grill at Colby's Hollow. Don't tell me you haven't been there yet."

"Okay, I won't tell you, but I didn't know there was *any*thing at Colby's Hollow besides a few houses and a church."

Romy laughed. "It's across the line into a wet county, so of course, there's a bar. I'll pick you up in a few minutes."

"I'll be ready."

Corporal's was small, probably seating forty people if every barstool at the long mahogany counter was occupied. It also smelled heavenly. The scent of tacos and their fixings was a guaranteed mood-builder.

"Not only tacos," Romy said, leading the way to a table near the fireplace, "but the best ones this side of Texas and the best-kept secret in Eastern Kentucky."

They ordered tacos and glasses of wine. "This is so nice," said Joss, looking around at the cozy little place. There was a peculiar absence of the beer signs she had expected to see. The omission wasn't a disappointment.

"It is." Romy sipped, then smiled across the table. "Speaking of Ez."

"We weren't."

"Yeah, I never talk about Seven, either."

Joss laughed. "Sure, you do. You just don't always do it aloud."

"Right."

Joss understood. She knew whatever story Romy and Seven shared, it lay unfinished in Romy's mind. Much like the story of Joss and Ez that had just started in Joss's.

And maybe finished. The thought made her shake her head. "I'm not ready," she said, "but I'm not sure what it is I'm not ready for. However, I do have a question you'll have an answer for. I need a house to rent."

"Sure."

The answer came quicker than Joss expected. She raised an eyebrow. "Are you a realtor, too? I know most everyone in Banjo Bend works more than one job, but I didn't know about that one."

"We haven't progressed to the point of having realtors yet, but my parents' house is empty."

"No one lives in it?"

"The last renter moved out a few weeks ago. It's right in Banjo Bend. If you like, we can go see it when we're done here."

Joss took a sip of crisp white zinfandel. "I'd like that." What she'd like, she realized, was to live in a house she wouldn't have to leave anytime soon. Although she liked the farmhouse and loved the memories that had accompanied her through painting its rooms, she'd never lost sight of the fact that her residency came with an expiration date. "We always talk about me," she said, "or it seems to me we do. I know you've been married, and now you're not, and that you own Romy's Place. That's not a lot to know almost three months into a friendship. What else? What's your favorite color? Your favorite flower?"

"Green. Wild ones. I got married in my twenties to a biker who came through town. He was looking for love and I was looking for a good time—we both got what we wanted. After a few years, though, he didn't want the love anymore, and I wasn't having a good time. We're still friends. He drives over the road and stops in whenever he's on a Lexington run." Regret slipped across Romy's face, instantly replaced with a smile. "He shows me pictures of his wife and kids, and I send him on his way with pie and coffee."

"Regrets?"

"A few. I kept thinking there was time to have kids until there wasn't. I thought I'd marry again because...you know, I liked it. I liked that kind of belonging to someone, but that's not enough reason to marry someone."

Joss thought of her marriage. It had undoubtedly occurred because her husband had been convinced—probably by his parents—that it was the right thing to do. All the plans had been made, her dress bought and altered, the hefty down payment that had been their wedding gift made on the house in Dolan Station.

Had she even been there? The thought was enough to make Joss's throat catch so that she couldn't speak. She'd been young, yes—only twenty to Brett's twenty-two—but had she also been completely stupid? Why was everything so brilliantly obvious in hindsight? "What's a good reason?" Her voice sounded as if it was coming through a cheese grater. "Everyone thinks theirs is the right one, yet half the time they're wrong. Half the time, Romy."

"And we were in the half that was wrong. Is that what you're thinking?" Romy shook her head. "I wouldn't give up a single day I spent with the biker, although by the time it ended, I was hating most of them. Your life with Brett, my friend, is over. From what you've said, it was probably over a while before you were forced to realize it. But it was a good life— don't waste time regretting it."

Joss finished her wine, thinking it had gone down very smoothly and a little faster than she was accustomed to. "You're right. I think between you and June and Margaret, I'm going to become a grownup." She laughed, actually feeling the joy in it. "One of the things that worried me—a lot—when I came here was that I was going to miss my girlfriends. I do, but have I ever been the lucky one since I got here."

After another glass of wine for Joss and an embarrassing number of tacos for each of them, they drove into Banjo Bend, taking the back road.

"It was a company house at one time." Romy turned onto one of the pretty little streets that spoked out from the park. "One that a foreman lived in or something—it wasn't one of the shotgun houses down by the creek. My dad bought it by paying the back taxes, and he and Mom moved there when they retired. It's little and cozy and not what you'd call convenient."

Joss loved the house. Its rooms were small—no self-respecting couch would fit in the living room and the dining room was no larger than her closet had been in Dolan Station. Closing the bathroom door was a necessity beyond privacy concerns because that was the only way you could get to the shower. An adorable half-bath was under the stairs; Joss could stand in it just fine, but anyone much taller than her five foot three would have banged their head. "Oh," she said, standing in the middle of the kitchen and turning around. "I love this, Romy."

She'd make the dining room into a library—she'd always wanted one. Brett had thought the idea was ridiculous, but it wasn't. It wasn't. None of the three bedrooms could accommodate a bed bigger than a queen, but that didn't matter—she wasn't sharing.

Her list of life questions didn't have many answers yet. She wasn't sure how she felt about Brett, about Cassie, or about Ez. She didn't know if the friendships she'd formed since coming to the Creek were of the forever kind.

But she knew this house was meant for her.

****

Ez twisted the pipe wrench around the drain beneath the bathroom sink in Cabin Ten. He felt as if he'd lost something he hadn't quite had. Granted, the little brick house on Dixon Avenue was only a couple of miles away from the campground, and he couldn't blame Joss for wanting a place she wouldn't have to move out of every time someone wanted to spend a weekend. But he liked stopping in to see her wherever she was working. He could still do that, he guessed, but it would be different once she moved. She probably wouldn't appear at every event that took place at the pavilion or join him on a last walk around the campground before calling it a night.

"It's okay if I stay in the farmhouse until after Thanksgiving, isn't it?" she asked.

They were replacing the first of the bathroom vanities he was certain the previous owner had built from cardboard boxes. "Of course, it is. That's where you're having your reunion." Under the sink, he got a face full of water and cursed mildly. "Hand me the—" A dry shop towel appeared as if by magic. "Thank you."

"You're welcome. The nice thing is that Thanksgiving weekend will be a test run of how the house will operate as a vacation home. Of course, there won't be any little kids staying there to stop up the toilets or jump off the porch roof wearing towels for capes, but—"

"What?" He pushed himself out from under the sink. "What are you talking about?"

She rolled her eyes. "Didn't you ever? Jump off a porch roof, I mean?"

"Only our own, and only until I got caught." That had been a painful experience. He wondered if Silas... "I guess that's why I needed more insurance." He wiped the rest of the water from his face and squinted. "Do you really think people will let their kids do that?"

"I suppose some will. I never let my kids do a lot of things, but as soon as I turned my back, they did them anyway. I kind of liked them that way." She grinned. "And I have a sneaking suspicion you were the same way."

He remembered, with an unexpected rush of pleasure, that he had been, and so had his brother. "Maybe we should put one of those jungle gym things in the backyard of the house."

"No need. The one up near the pavilion is great and close enough." She put the tools he'd used back in the box and set about cleaning the new vanity. "These will look nice. Much better than what was there."

He nodded. "You'll end up having to touch up the paint around them. I'm sorry about that. I should have thought of it before."

They cleaned up after themselves and left the cabin. With the toolbox once more loaded into the back of the utility vehicle, he drove to the next one. "Why don't you plan to stay until the first of the year if no one rents the farmhouse?" he suggested. "That'll give you an even day with your rent and give you time to finish un-whiting every room in the house you're moving into."

"Okay. Thank you."

"You're going to keep working here, aren't you?" He knew he asked the question awkwardly, but he needed to know. "You don't have to, but you and Margaret and Wil make a really good winter crew. Plus Jed will be here weekends."

"I'd like to."

"Do you want some help painting your house?" He asked because she was still putting in quite a few hours at the campground. She worked fast, but as small as the brick house she'd rented was, it had a lot of nooks and crannies.

"Yes." She beamed. "I'm having a painting party Thursday. I'd love to have you come. Pizza and beer provided."

Oh, a party. Not his kind of thing. Definitely not in so confined of a space. Maybe he could…well, no, he couldn't. He'd offered, and he could live with one day of socializing. "Do I see a scaffold and some ceilings in my future?"

"Oh, I do hope so." He watched as she walked ahead, admiring how well she filled out a pair of jeans and a campgrounds sweatshirt.

At the door of the cabin, she turned. "Are you coming, or is installing vanities part of my job description now?"

"You never can tell. Could be." He stepped onto the porch and put his arm around her as he unlocked the door. He hadn't really meant to, but she was right there and smelled good. He liked her more than was good for him, that was for dang sure. He was relieved she was staying. That was sure, too.

Chapter Eleven

Sister June Esther arrived on Tuesday night before Thanksgiving, taking her bag up to the same room she'd used the last time and re-emerging in the kitchen a few minutes later with her rolling pin. "It was Gran's." She held it up. "I can't make piecrust without it, but if you want me to leave it here in the house I will."

Joss loved to bake, but she couldn't make piecrust at all. She bought the roll-up kind out of the dairy case at the supermarket, but she saw no reason to mention that. "You keep it," she said generously. "What kind are we having?"

June rolled her eyes. "Duh. It's Thanksgiving. Pumpkin and pecan."

Even with June's comforting presence, Joss spent Wednesday morning having second thoughts about the gathering. And seventieth thoughts. She didn't want to look like an idiot, but it had been so long since she'd seen Gray…even longer since she'd seen Seven. What if they didn't like her anymore? It *hadn't* been that long since she'd seen Cassie and Brett, and she *knew* they didn't like her. Why were they coming anyway? The boys couldn't, and Brett had never had any fondness for her cousins. Their acceptance RSVP had been a shock she was still reeling from.

Sipping her coffee and gazing out the window, Joss

had her seventy-first thought and sniffed the air, fancying she could already smell the pies June hadn't baked yet. She willed herself to stop overthinking everything. This holiday wasn't about the Joss-Brett-Cassie triangle; rather, it was about a family get-together, the first one in too many years.

She set the flour and sugar canisters—big, glass candy jars rescued years before from the old general store building in Colby's Hollow—on the long table in the kitchen. How many times had the girl cousins baked in this room with Gran? Never the boys—they gagged at the very idea—but they were always around when the oven timer went off.

When she'd put staples away when she moved in, she arranged them as her grandmother had. The spices were all in the wooden tray that had been a gift from the local grain elevator, with the brown sugar sealed in a smaller candy jar. She'd found the things in both the attic and the basement and put them back into use. The measuring cups and spoons, incongruously new colorful ones, were Joss's own. Gran never used them.

"I'm so surprised you're leaving this house when you've done such a good job of making it feel the way it did when we were kids." June's voice came from the bottom of the stairs as she stepped into the kitchen.

"It's nice being here, isn't it?" Joss felt an embarrassing wave of pride in herself for what she'd accomplished. "At first, the idea of moving out of it no sooner than it was done just killed me, but it's not a 'me' house at all, no matter how much I love it. I may not know what else I'm doing in this second act I'm intent on, but I do know I want a house that reflects who I am." She grinned, lifting her cup in a mocking self-toast. "May I eventually figure out who that is."

"You will."

By the time the sun was up, pies were in the oven, and Joss had potatoes cooking for potato salad and was making the cranberry salad. "Are you *sure* anyone likes it?" she asked, grimacing at the cranberry, orange, and pecan mixture. "I'd just as soon make juice with the oranges, eat the pecans, and throw the cranberries into the woods for the birds."

"Marley loves it, and I think one of the boys does, too."

"Oh, well, then." If Marley loved it, that was good enough for Joss. She wondered momentarily if Ez liked it, and heat crept up her face. What difference did it make what he liked? This was one meal, for heaven's sake. Well, probably two. They always ate dinner and then, later in the day, filled the table again and had supper from the leftovers.

Thanksgiving was going to be fun. She was determined it would be. She'd invited Cady Whittier and Wyatt Iverson, both transplants to Banjo Bend. Just as in Gran's days, the number expected was hard to gauge, but the food would be plentiful, and no one had ever been harmed by sitting on the floor.

"When are people going to be here?" asked June.

"Your parents and Gray's are coming in tonight. They're all staying in Banjo Bend—the motel's open for the weekend. Gray will be here this afternoon, I think, and Cassie and Brett tomorrow. I don't know about Seven."

"He's coming with Gray. They're both flying into Lexington. I was supposed to tell you that and forgot." June shook her head. "It's been so long since Seven's talked to any of us that he may just sit and text me, even when we're all together."

"You think he and Ez will compete for who's the most reclusive?"

"It could happen. What will you do if it does?"

Joss laughed, surprised at the question. "I'm not doing anything. They're grownups."

"There you go."

The gentle answer made her look over at where her cousin was pulling pies from the oven. "What do you mean?"

"That's what you need to remember, even when my parents and Gray's are bossing us around—that we're all grownups. If Brett ends up acting like he's an authority figure, you can tell him to step down. You don't have to do or say anything you don't want to."

"You're right." Joss put plastic wrap over the disgusting salad and stuck it in the fridge, considering. "But I will admit to being glad my mother decided not to come." She wasn't going to address the idea of Brett as an authority figure. She didn't think they'd had that kind of marriage. She certainly hoped not.

Joss and June went into town and had lunch with Marley, promising to pick her up "tomorrow" and that she would be glad to see the "big boys" she couldn't seem to remember. After coffee with Romy at the café, they drove into the next county and replenished the beer and soda supply and made a stop at the local winery before returning to the farmhouse.

By the time the tap came at the front door that afternoon, the house smelled wonderful. The beds were all made, and towels hung in the bathrooms. Joss's heart felt as if it would burst through her chest as she flung open the door and stood with her hands on her hips and a dishtowel over her shoulder. "Who do you think you are, using the front door?"

Long arms came around her and held long and hard, and she returned the embrace, moisture stinging her eyes. "Oh, Gray, I've missed you."

He was still tall, lanky, and gorgeous. His hair was still long and thick, and if there was any gray in its strands, Joss couldn't see it. Behind glasses, his Murphy blue eyes sparkled and danced. She hugged him again.

"I've missed you, too." He reached for June. "And you."

Joss stepped past Gray and June to look into the eyes of the man who stood silently just inside the door. Other than the dark red hair that matched her own—only his was straight, something she'd never quite forgiven him for—no sign of Murphy appeared in him. His father had been of Native American descent, and it showed in Seven's high cheekbones and straight, thin nose. Although he was forty-seven, there was no softening in his jaw line, and no wrinkles anywhere.

If she hadn't been so glad to see him, she might have resented that. "Sev." She was uncertain whether she could hug him as she had Gray. He'd never welcomed physical affection, even from his mother.

But it had been so long. "Sev," she said again, and put her arms around him.

He hugged her back, but released her quickly. "Thanks for asking me, Joss. It's good to see you."

"Thank you for the flowers."

He nodded. "How are you doing?"

"Fine." She was, too, more every day. Better on

ones when she saw Ezra McIntire, but she wasn't going there now. This weekend was about family, not mid-life crushes.

When Seven moved on to greet June, Gray grinned past them at Joss. "Got beer?"

"We do." She led the way toward the kitchen, calling over her shoulder. "You want a beer, too, Seven?"

"Sure. Thanks." He brought up the rear, looking around as if trying to take it all in.

She saw him, caught what might have been longing in his eyes. "Why don't you guys bring your stuff in and look around the house first? You can fight over the two bedrooms in the back—June called dibs on the front one, and I've got Gran's. We'll wait down here and keep the beer cold for you."

When the "boy cousins" had brought in their bags and carried them upstairs, June nodded. "Good move, cuz, letting them get back to feeling at home."

"They look so good, don't they?"

"They do."

By the time Joss and June had set out the cheese and crackers that were an afternoon staple item and poured healthy glasses of pinot grigio for themselves, Gray and Seven were coming down the stairs. They made as much noise as they had thirty-five years ago, and Joss laughed, delighted with the memory.

"Is Ez coming around today?" Gray helped himself to a beer and handed Seven one. "This will never get us through tomorrow." He frowned at the row of bottles still on the shelf.

"No, but what's in the fridge on the back porch will, or we're going to need an intervention." Joss sat at the end of the long table, and the others joined her. "I don't know if Ez is stopping by today or not. Text him if you like."

Catching up was, as Joss had feared, awkward at first. Although they'd been together at Gran's funeral, the time had been short and grief-filled. In some ways, it was like being with strangers. Beloved strangers.

"Okay." June took off her watch. "Thirty seconds apiece or a whole minute? We'll catch up with each other, and then we'll all be comfortable again. Right?"

"Sounds good." Gray, always the gregarious leader of the pack, cleared his throat. "I'll go first."

They knew then, much more than a half minute later, that he was still a diplomat but had curtailed his world travel because he had finally tired of it. He was at a turning point in his life but wasn't sure which direction to head... "Although I like the idea of going into old age as a drummer in a rock band." He'd never married again, still kept contact with Millie, and regretted that he didn't have kids because he knew his progeny would have been better than anyone else's, no matter how Joss felt about her twins. He ended at the same time his beer did, and he got another one.

They all laughed at his monologue. At least Joss and June did. Seven just smiled, his gaze thoughtful on his male cousin. As she looked into Gray's eyes, Joss understood Seven's look. Something was undoubtedly not right with Gray.

"I'm next." June lifted her glass in salute and reset the timer on her watch. "I'm taking a whole minute so I can talk for Marley, too." She took a deep breath, then fell silent for a full five seconds. "Come on, you guys, I'm a nun. How much of a story can I have?"

Joss knew she could have more than she told, although what she did relate was interesting.

The kitchen and shelter she was a part of answered her need to help others. She was ready, she thought, to move on from it, but, like Gray, wasn't sure which direction to move. "That's up to the Lord, I believe, and He's not letting me in on His thoughts."

Ez came in while she was talking.

Joss saw him from the corner of her eye and realized he must have knocked, but no one heard him. She smiled in welcome and he smiled back but didn't interrupt June.

"Marley's losing ground." June had to stop, her voice failing.

Gray put his arm around her, pulling her to him. "Ah, Junie." His voice was soft. "Never in her heart or her soul. They're bigger and brighter than any of the rest of us can claim."

June sniffed, accepting the tissue Seven offered. "We knew it would happen, just not when. The good thing is that she doesn't *know* she's failing, just that she's tired. Any sign of pain and she's given more medication. She sleeps a great deal, but when she's awake, she's completely herself. Still rainbows and butterflies. She still thinks only in terms of yesterday and tomorrow. She'll be glad to see you tomorrow, but she won't remember it on Friday." She stopped the timer. "That's all."

Seven spoke quietly into the silence. "It will be good to see her."

Gray nodded, then looked toward where the light in the room had changed a minute before. "Ez." He got up, going to where Ez stood inside the door.

They said very little, although their handshake was a long one, their searching gazes even longer. Gray introduced Ez and Seven, then returned to his seat. "We're catching up. It's Joss's turn, or Seven's."

Joss was up, preparing to offer Ez a beer, but he shook his head. He was carrying the heavy glass he always drank bourbon out of. She returned to her seat and he took the chair beside hers, lifting a cracker and a slice of gouda off her plate without asking.

She liked that he didn't ask. "Sev?" She smiled across the table, still almost unbelieving he was here.

He looked for a moment at the timer on the table before saying, "I live in Atlantic City. I own half of a casino there." He hesitated. "We used to talk about what we wanted to be when we grew up. What we wanted our lives to be. I still don't know. There you have it."

"No marriage? No kids?" Joss squinted across the table at him. It was obvious Seven didn't want to talk about his life, but surely he hadn't spent the last thirty-some years in a casino, had he?

Seven met her gaze, his own expression so dispassionate it was chilling. "Married once. She died."

The pain buried deep in his voice took her breath away. "I'm sorry." She could see by their faces that June and Gray hadn't known, either, and she wondered why, but things had always been that way with Seven. As much a part of them as he was, he'd held himself separate, too.

He looked around at the group, his mouth lifting in a slight smile. "I'm all right." He lifted his bottle. "Except that this is empty, and it is exceptionally good beer. Local?"

"It is." Ez nodded. "There are several microbreweries in the area—that one's the best."

"I can believe that." Seven went to the refrigerator for another bottle, then stepped to the back door, standing stiff and quiet for a minute as he gazed back onto the darkening woods.

Joss saw the slight slump of his broad shoulders when he relaxed, felt the release of tension, and understood how difficult his disclosure had been. "My turn," she said briskly, "and since my life's pretty much an open book, I'll just say some pages have been torn out of it in the past year or so. That the twins are understandably remarkable when you remember who their mother is. That I'm referring to life in the moment as Act Two." She met Ez's eyes for an instant, sharing something sweetly intimate. "That I'm having a really good time."

****

He hadn't expected to be next. This timer business was a family thing, wasn't it? They were just trying to catch up on what they'd missed over the years. He and Silas did the same thing on their rare phone calls. "You doing okay?" one would ask, and the other would say, "You bet. You?"

"No, man, I want to know." Gray leaned an elbow on the table and grinned, the expression wicked. "I may be compelled to share some of what I know about Naval Air Station Pensacola and training days if you don't enlighten us about the years since."

Ez shrugged. He could do a half minute. He'd make Gray pay later, but he could share. Some. "Flew helicopters. Retired from the navy. Got my doctorate. Taught social statistics at a college in Virginia. Had an…experience there. PT—"

He stopped, just long enough for the pause to be noticeable, for people to turn their heads sharply in his direction. Cursing himself for nearly saying more than he'd intended, he went on, "Left there and bought a campground on the recommendation of my old friend, the drummer. Been losing money hand over fist ever since but have finally learned all the words to 'The Wreck of the Edmund Fitzgerald.' I've also cut my time for completing the *New York Times* crossword considerably." He took a deep swallow of bourbon and soda, thinking he should make some excuses and go home. This was a family gathering, and he had no place in it.

"Let's take a walk." June got up abruptly, removing empty beer bottles and plates from the table. "We're having pizza for supper, and we need to make room for it. You guys need to see the campground anyway. Sometimes it feels as if Gran and Granddad are still here. You mind giving us all the nickel tour, Ez?"

"Not at all." He was surprised to find that he meant it. He appreciated that Joss and June liked the direction their grandparents' farm had taken. He was interested in hearing what Gray and Seven thought.

Walking through the woods in the snow was like being back in high school, going to ice skate on the pond behind the barn where they used to shoot baskets. Gray, who'd lived in a warm climate most of his adult life, complained mightily about the cold the whole way. He stepped on a patch of ice as they approached the pavilion and fell, looking almost poetic in the motion.

Joss and June ran to make sure he was all right, but

151

Ez and Seven doubled over laughing, leaning against trees to keep from joining Gray in lying-down mode.

Gray got to his feet, making use of Joss's arm and June's hand. He brushed snow off his coat and pants and nodded toward where Seven was leaning forward with his hands on his knees and Ez was wiping at the tears streaming from his eyes. They were still laughing. Without raising his voice, Gray called them a string of names that should have turned the air blue.

Joss whapped her cousin's shoulder. "What would Gran say? Shame on you."

Gray sniffed, giving his head a toss. "She'd say they deserved it."

June waved a dismissive hand. "In your dreams." She gave him a push. "Go up there and look at the pavilion. It's on the footprint of the tobacco barn, but it's been enlarged beyond it."

Ez hung back a little. What the Murphy cousins thought of the campground mattered more to him than he was comfortable with. He'd somehow become the caretaker for their growing-up memories. He wasn't sure how it had happened, but he hoped he'd done it right.

"Is there any chance we could have a fire?" Seven's voice was quieter than Gray's, and yet it carried well.

Ez moved forward. "Sure. The fire's always laid. Of course, we can't have Gray playing with matches." He unlocked the storage locker and got a few firelighters and five lightweight Adirondack chairs out. "Sorry, no marshmallows in there."

The fire lit instantly, which meant Jed had laid it. The kid definitely had a touch with anything found in nature, even manmade things.

They settled into the seats in a curved line around the hearth. Although they tried to include him in the conversation, the cousins' talk centered around their memories of being on this land years before. Their memories were different, just as his and Silas's undoubtedly were, but held together with common threads. They'd all loved their grandparents and what they'd learned from them.

"I swear I was the only woman in Dolan Station who could drive a stick shift." Joss mimicked shifting three-on-a-tree. "Well, the only one I knew, anyway."

"At least you could drive one." Seven spoke from the end chair. "As I recall, June just stripped gears—she didn't actually drive."

"Your memory is" —June hesitated, giving him a reasonable facsimile of Gran's stink-eye— "excrement, cuz. I saw absolutely no reason to bother with second gear, that's all. And occasionally third, if it was a four-speed."

"She's right." Gray leaned forward to nod in Seven's direction. "You wouldn't remember that because you were…what shall we say?…impaired? Yes, that was it."

Seven snorted. "As if you'd know."

"Ez could have written the book on impairment." Gray grinned at Ez. "Other people's, anyway. I swear, he was the designated driver everywhere we went."

He had been, too. Although Ez liked to drink, he didn't often do it away from home—he never had. Even at Pensacola, the urge to protect had been overdeveloped. His military comrades hadn't needed him for that—at least not in the days Gray was referring to. Later on, yeah.

And he'd failed them.

He stirred in the chair, wanting the subject to change before he went down the despair road again. "Did you guys stay here all summer when you were kids?" He looked down the curved row of cousins. "Some of you lived right in Banjo Bend, didn't you?"

"All of us did except Joss and Cassie," said June, "but most of our parents worked during the day, so they were happy to have us at the farm. Sometimes we went home, but more often, we just stayed with Gran and Granddad. When we got old enough to stay by ourselves, we still spent summers at the farm." She smiled, the expression both sweet and sad. "It would have been so easy for me to resent having to take care of Marley, because, you know, I did most of the time. But when we were out here, Gran was the chief caregiver. It gave me time to just be a kid, plus I learned from her the right things to do."

"We all learned from her." Seven's voice was quiet. "You all knew I gambled, and that I was lucky, and that Gran worried about it. What you didn't know was that she taught me to play poker one winter when my mom…one winter. Gran used to tell me if I got killed in a dark alley by someone I'd beaten, she'd feel responsible." He smiled, his lean face gentling. "I've made it a practice to stay out of dark alleys."

Soon, Ez and Gray walked to his house to gather more to drink and order pizza to be delivered to the pavilion. They drove back in the UTV and pulled a picnic table close to the fire.

Somewhere in the woods, coming from the direction of Colby's Hollow, gunfire sounded, cracking loud even in the muffling snow. Ez tried not to stiffen but knew he'd failed when Joss's hand clasped his fingers, and Gray's gaze found his across the table.

"Hunters?" Seven tipped his head to one side, listening.

"Yeah." Ez took a couple of deep breaths. "Did you guys hunt back then?"

Joss shook her head, her fingers warm around his hand, rubbing gently. "Granddad taught us all to shoot, because he thought it was something we needed to know, but there wasn't a hunter among us."

"Because if we shot anything, we had to take care of it," said Gray. "Make sure it was dead, then skin it and take the meat to people who ate it—we didn't."

"Unlike fish, which we caught, cleaned, *and* ate." June held up her hands. "Were it not for that wicked filet knife, I'm sure I could have made it as a hand model instead of a nun."

Gray snickered. "Except for Cassie. She was okay with the fishing part, but she for sure wasn't going to clean one. I don't think she ever did, did she?"

"She only liked fishing until she found out she wasn't good at it." June shook her head. "Unlike Seven and poker."

"I think that's a gene that missed me." Joss sipped from an insulated wineglass. "If I only did things I was good at, I wouldn't do much."

Ez frowned at her. "You're good at lots of things."

She grinned. "No, I just *do* lots of things. I'm good at choosing colors, but I'm mediocre at painting. You don't want to look real close."

"You're a good friend." Seven picked up her hand and squeezed it. He sat on the other side of Joss, and he met Ez's eyes over her head. The glance wasn't unfriendly, really, more like a warning.

Ez recognized the signs of another perpetual caretaker. Someone else who felt responsible, even when he wasn't. "I agree with Seven, and if you're going to be good at something, I'll take that." He hoped he gave to the friendship, too, but that might be something to think about later, when he had less alcohol in his system.

He wondered if Seven Murphy's calm was as expensive as his own, if he'd learned watchfulness because of not having been vigilant when he should have been.

They finally let the fire burn down shortly after midnight. They put the chairs back into the storage cabinet, leaving the picnic table where it was. He had a feeling Murphys would be back up here by the time the weekend was over.

Having them here was nice. Not just for Joss, although he liked seeing her so happy, but for himself, too. Knowing that for all his gregariousness, Gray Douglas was watchful. He was also probably the best friend Ez had ever had. "I'm doing a last drive-through," he said when everyone was preparing to walk back to the farmhouse. "There are college kids in some of the motor homes, and they get noisy sometimes." He met Joss's gaze, and consciousness of the others in the group fell away, becoming like the background in a photograph. "Do you want to ride along?"

"Yes."

Gray gave June a gentle elbow. "You notice he didn't ask us."

"I did notice." She tucked her hand through the

elbow that had just pushed against her. "I'm not taking that personally, but maybe you should."

"He should." Ez nodded at June. "You want to explain that to him?"

She laughed. "No. I don't have all night. Sev, you ready? Let's take him back to the house."

The three of them walked off together, Gray gesticulating and Seven's low voice responding.

Ez reached for Joss's hand. "Want to take the long way around the park, or are you cold?"

"Let's go the long way."

They drove slowly. Ez held her hand against his leg. "Your cousin…the one I hadn't met before…he seems like a good guy."

"He does, doesn't he? I was so afraid I wouldn't know him anymore—it had been so long. I talked to Gray, even video-chatted with him. But until Seven sent me flowers after my divorce, I never heard from him. I didn't even know where he was until June told me."

"Are you excited about tomorrow? Seeing your aunts and uncles and having the house full of people?"

"Yes. And a little worried about seeing my ex and my sister. But ripping off that bandage now is better than standing around at someone's funeral having regrets, isn't it?"

He thought it probably was, but he was cognizant of the nervousness that threaded through her voice. "You'll be among friends," he said. "I expect they'll be more uncomfortable than you are, because they have reason—you don't. I think it's one of those high road, low road things we learned about when we were kids. You're taking the high one."

"For selfish reasons. Because I like being the good

guy and so my kids can have good relationships with their dad and their aunt. Not too noble of me, I'm afraid."

"Noble enough." He drew the vehicle to a stop to look out at the creek, calm and silvered by the moon and surrounded by the melting snow. "Looking out at that makes me wish I was an artist."

"Me, too."

He laid his arm across her shoulders, and she leaned into him, the softness of her hair tickling his chin.

Deep in the woods, gunshots sounded again. Although he stiffened, Ez didn't jump. Joss's hand slipped into his. They didn't say anything.

Chapter Twelve

The house was full by eleven o'clock on Thanksgiving morning. Joss was excited by seeing Gray's parents, Aunt Leah and Uncle Perry, and June and Marley's parents, Aunt Eileen and Uncle Dave, whom she hadn't seen since Gran's funeral.

Marley, who June and Gray picked up earlier, was having a good day. She was thrilled to see everyone and remembered all their names, even though she hadn't seen them since "yesterday."

The arrival of Brett and Cassie was blessedly anticlimactic. Joss, directing the movement of furniture to accommodate the portable digital piano Eileen brought, met her sister's eyes when they came in. She smiled, nodded, and went back to the kitchen.

The aunts, delighted to see friends and family who hadn't been together in this house for so many years, had slipped easily into hostess roles.

Joss was glad for it. She'd always been a better cook than entertainer. She didn't smile at Brett, but she didn't jerk away from the one-armed hug he greeted her with, either. How odd, though, that his touch was no longer familiar.

"You look good," he said quietly.

"Thank you." He did, too, probably because he was happy. She thought the time might come when she'd be glad for him. Maybe.

Ez was almost the last to arrive, coming in the back door carrying his guitar case, then going back out to help Romy carry in the ham and the turkey she'd roasted at the café that morning.

Uncle Dave, being the senior Murphy in attendance, carved the turkey, using Gran's carving knife that had come from Arizona with Gray's parents. Everyone crowded into the kitchen to watch and give directions.

"I worried the whole way here." Aunt Leah shook her head at her own concern. "We had to check it at the airport, of course, and I just knew it would be in the only piece of luggage to be forever lost. Mama would have haunted me."

"She would, too." Dave brandished the old knife dramatically before laying its blade against the turkey. He scowled at Leah. "Even though she always liked you best."

"She did not." She waved a dismissive hand at her brother. "After the kids were born, she didn't like any of us anymore, just them."

He nodded, the merriment in his eyes belying his sad expression. "True enough."

"Just Gray and me, Uncle Dave," said Seven. "She didn't really like the girls that much."

"Geeze, Sev"—Gray's voice rose, scandalized— "do you have to tell everything you know? They had no idea."

"You do forget, Seven dear, that there are twice as many of us." June patted his cheek, maybe a little hard—more like a slap. "We can probably take you."

"Guaranteed you can take him," said Gray, "because I'm hiding under the table."

Ez, who'd been mostly silent since he arrived, lifted an eyebrow. "Again?"

Gray spoke into the laughter that followed. "Yeah, but there's plenty of room under there for you and Seven, too."

"You children behave." Aunt Eileen rapped the heads of every "child" she could reach from where she was arranging the stack of plates and baskets of silverware. "Joss, where did you find all these plates? I know your grandmother was always prepared to feed the masses, but surely these weren't all in the attic."

Joss grinned at Wyatt. "More came from the Banjo Bend Community Church. Its pastor, I learned, is open to bribery."

"As is any pastor of a small church, especially single ones who don't cook well," said Wyatt piously.

Joss looked around at the guests, her heart full. "The family knife has officially been turned back over to Aunt Leah for safekeeping. Will you say grace before we start, Wyatt?"

More than twenty people in Gran's kitchen qualified as a crowd, but they all managed to fit in and clasp hands. Joss held Ez's on one side and Cassie's on the other. Her sister's small fingers, mirror images of her own, curled around hers. Cassie's eyes, green like their mother's instead of Murphy blue, met hers and filled with tears.

Joss swallowed hard and squeezed her sister's hand.

The meal was loud and long, punctuated by Aunt Eileen's worried "I hope there's enough," which someone has said at absolutely every family meal ever prepared on earth. The "boys" tossed the dinner rolls when anyone asked for one, and Uncle Perry threatened to box all their ears, including the ones who weren't related to him.

Joss took seconds of Aunt Eileen's dressing. "I've got to have the recipe for this. I won't make it, but I'll think about it a lot."

"It's in your gran's cookbook," said Eileen. "Along with notes about how much to make so there is enough to be eating leftovers at least until Christmas."

"That cookbook has that eggplant recipe in it." Cassie shuddered. "Remember? It was the first and last time I ever ate eggplant. I don't know how anything could be such a pretty color and still taste so terrible."

"That's the only thing we ever all agreed on," said June. "Even Marley wouldn't eat it."

Leah nodded. "There's a big X through it in the book."

After the meal, Joss emptied the dishwasher and reloaded it while the other women moved the leftovers into smaller receptacles and covered them. Then they washed the rest of the dishes, coming together around the table with cups of coffee. The men had divided into two groups—half going to watch football in the family room, the other half playing music in the living room.

Marley, tired from the excitement of the day, lay on Joss's bed. Aunt Eileen tucked her in and came back to the kitchen, tears slipping silently down her face. "She was asleep almost before I'd covered her." Her voice cracked.

Leah put her arm around her sister-in-law, drawing her into a hug. "You did a good thing bringing us together today, Joss. I don't know why we got out of the habit after Mama died, but we did. It's good to be back here, to feel this place again, and to spend time with each other."

"I so appreciate being invited, too," said Cady. The pretty librarian had been quiet, although she and Jed had talked a lot and sat together at the table. She smiled shyly. "You all have made me feel like family."

June smiled at her. "We're glad you came."

"Where are you from, Cady?" asked Eileen.

"I'm an army brat, so I'm not really from anywhere, but my parents settled in Texas after they retired from the military. It's too hot there for me, and I loved it here when we visited one year, so when Banjo Bend's library showed up in job listings, I grabbed it."

Cady and Jed both left early.

Joss packed containers of leftovers for them and hugged them both goodbye, feeling very Gran-like and mellow.

The women walked together late in the afternoon, laughing at the separation-by-gender that never seemed to change at family gatherings. "I used to think it was purely sexist when it happened," said Joss. "It took having my own kitchen to figure out that men—the ones I knew anyway—just got in the way when it was crowd cooking."

"They do." Aunt Leah nodded. "But I think they do it on purpose so they can go hold down the couch and drink beer and watch football."

Her sister-in-law nodded. "It might be generational, too. The younger ones all seem to be making music. Except for Brett."

"Brett likes football," said Cassie. "Not music so much. Except for the symphony sometimes, and we go to see the big names at the Opry."

Her tone was defensive, and Joss remembered feeling that way when she was trying to convince people her husband wasn't a snob. He was. Not an intentional one, perhaps, but a social elitist nonetheless.

"He helps in the kitchen a lot at home," Cassie continued. "He never gets in the way."

No one seemed to know what to say for a minute, then Leah asked, "How's your mother, Cassie? Doing well, I hope."

"Yes, she's fine. She's spending the holiday with friends."

"Be sure to give her our best." Eileen's request was quiet.

Joss stepped between her aunts so she could hug them both. They had no reason to be kind to her mother, but would be that way to the death anyway; to them, she was still family.

"Thank you." Cassie drew a breath, so deep it shuddered as she released it. "And thank you for doing this, Joss, for inviting Brett and me. I'm sure it wasn't easy." She hesitated. "How do you know Cady?"

"Just from the library. I go every week, so I see her there, plus I think she and Jed are seeing each other, and he's at the campground all the time. She's sweet, isn't she?" said Joss.

Cassie nodded.

"Her hair reminded me of yours." *When we were young.* Cassie's wasn't golden and curly anymore. It was platinum, worn in a curving-under swing around her shoulders. Her natural beauty had segued into out-and-out glamour. She seemed brittle. Or maybe that was just what Joss wanted to think.

When the women returned from the walk to the

creek, it was time to set out the food and plates and silverware again. Marley had wakened from her nap and flirted with the "big boys" who were attending to her every need. They ate again, talking in a crowd around the long kitchen table, and then the crowd began to dissipate. Some would meet in the morning for Black Friday shopping. Romy would go back to work. Joss was taking Ez and the cousins to look at her rental house.

Margaret, promising to meet Leah and Eileen for shopping, left with Wil, and Joss and Ez shared a knowing smirk.

"I'm going home," he said quietly, when everyone was gone except the cousins who were staying in the house. "Have you had a good day?"

She brought his coat and her own. "I'll walk you out. Yes. Much better than I could have even hoped for. Were you bored with all the family reminiscences?"

He followed her onto the back porch. "No. Although I got lost sometimes. No one mention's Seven's parents. Was he adopted?"

"No. Aunt Dorie, his mother, was my dad's sister. She evidently left home after a falling-out with Granddad and came back a year or so later with a baby. She was—" Joss hesitated, not sure enough of her facts to tell Aunt Dorie's story "— troubled, and I think an addict. She and Seven lived in Banjo Bend, but she wasn't around much. I don't know who his father is, although I think he does. She died while we were in high school—she and Dad had the same heart disease and died within a year of each other. Granddad followed soon after. I think his heart was broken."

Ez shook his head. "That's rough. My mom died

165

when I was in high school, too. It changed everything. We still had the old man, although he'd have been happier if we hadn't been around."

"Seven enlisted after his junior year. He finished school in the army and never really came home again. He came to visit Gran, but no one else saw him. It's so good to see him now. His life's still a mystery, but there's a lot of the old Seven in him. He's still funny. Still smart."

"I think so, too. I like him."

They reached the road, and he stopped. "You need to go back to the house now," he said, "or I'll be walking you back. Thanks for inviting me. It was a really good day."

"Thanks for coming." She smiled up at him, feeling surrounded by his warmth even though they weren't touching. "See you later?"

He smiled back, then bent his head to touch his lips to hers, taking his time about kissing her. His arms linked around her, drawing her in.

She didn't want to be lost in the cloud of feeling that surrounded her as surely as his arms did…really, she didn't. She didn't want to be in love with someone ever again, especially not yet. Not when the bruises had just healed. Before she wanted to, she drew away.

He let her go, but his eyes were questioning. "How was it today? Seeing Brett and your sister, I mean? Or I am I crossing the line into minding your business?"

She shrugged. "Nothing private about it. I think Cassie and I made a fragile peace, which is the only kind of peace we've ever had, so it was all I could have hoped for. Seeing Brett was…weird. Because it was as if he was someone I never knew at all, just"—she interrupted herself with a laugh—"like Marley said, a 'grumpy big boy.' I think the biggest thing I felt was relief."

Saying it aloud made her feel it again. She looped her arms loosely around Ez's neck. If it was foolish to get lost in a sweet swirl of liking and more than a little lust this soon, so be it. "That's a big Thanksgiving thing for me."

He kissed her again, in answer, several times, a little longer and deeper each time. She kissed him back, her fingers in the warm silkiness of his hair. And she thought the swirl might just become a maelstrom, if she didn't go back into the house. "It's getting cold out here," she murmured, "and they're going to wonder what we're doing."

He chuckled. "No, they're not."

She bit his bottom lip lightly. "You're right, but Gray will make stuff up. You know he will."

"Did I just hear my name being taken in vain?" Gray's voice came from the porch as he stepped out the door, followed by Seven pulling on his coat. "I'm trying to make noise in case you two kids are up to something." He came to where they stood and gave Joss a tight, one-armed hug. "You did a good thing here today, cuz, just like Mom said."

"Did you interrupt us for some reason?" Ez gave him a fraternal push.

Gray pushed back. "Yeah. Seven and I thought we'd come to your house for a while. We wouldn't have to watch our language, and no one would be counting beer bottles. Sev said we hadn't been invited, but I told him it was just an oversight on your part, and we'd surely be welcome."

"Well, you're right—this time, anyway."

The pleasure in Ez's voice surprised Joss. She knew he and Gray were friends, but she'd have expected him to be yearning for alone time by now. "Oh, thank goodness," she said, clapping her hands. "Now June and I can drink and say whatever we want without worrying about boy cousins gossiping."

"Don't lock them out, though, Joss, or they'll end up in the tent camping section, stealing some kid's pup tent to sleep in. It's too cold for that."

He kissed her again, right in front of Gray and Seven. "I'll see you tomorrow."

"Goodnight." She smiled at him, joy pushing up inside her. She felt like dancing and would have if she hadn't had witnesses. That they saw the kiss was enough to leave her open to questions she didn't have answers to—a solo line dance up the sidewalk would make it worse. Inside, she hung up her coat and went back to her room to change into pajamas and Gran's robe. "You want hot chocolate?" she called, hearing June coming down the stairs.

"Yes, with a touch of something medicinal in it."

"Are nuns supposed to drink?"

"Did you not hear the word *medicinal*?"

They sat at the end of the table a few minutes later, sharing stories of the day. They worried together over Marley's failing health and Uncle Perry's cataracts, speculated shamelessly over Gray's and Seven's love lives, and skirted the subject of Brett. Joss thought that was fine—she didn't want to talk about him.

"Cassie's thin," June commented. "Too thin."

"Brett loves thin." Well, so much for not wanting to talk about him. "We used to talk about eating disorders—Noah had a girlfriend who was anorexic—and Brett just couldn't see where it was a real problem. He thought the thinner you were, the more controlled you were."

"And yet—" June stopped, lifting her cup to her lip. She didn't go on.

"And yet?" Joss prompted.

"He wanted to control you, didn't he?"

There it was, the biggest thing about her marriage she never wanted to face. The issue she walked around, danced around, and denied. She'd managed not to talk about it in the fourteen months since she and Brett had separated, and yet June just popped it right out there late on Thanksgiving night.

Tired from a long and busy day, her mood…changed…by the additive in her hot chocolate, Joss let down the last guard. "Not only wanted to, he *did* control me. The other part is that I let him, that I thought it was the way to maintain a successful marriage and that perfect life I liked so much. Did you know I took pictures of how the pillows were arranged on the sofa and the bed so that I could get them right every time? The shots are still on my phone."

"You're blaming yourself." June's voice was sharp. "Don't do that."

"Who *is* to blame?"

"Well, Brett, for one. Your mother, I think, although I have no business saying so, for another. The fact that she *couldn't* be pleased made you think the problem was with you. Your dad, lovely as he was, demonstrated until the day he died that it was easier just to let her have her way."

"Do you know how bad it feels," said Joss, holding

her eyes wide in the hopes that tears wouldn't escape them, "to be played like a damn fiddle your whole life?"

"I know that there are those of us who have to be what other people need them to be. I haven't taken enough psychology courses to explain that, but I know it's true. It's why I've always been Marley's caregiver—even before I became her legal guardian. It's probably the 'why' of other things, too. But, Jossie" —June captured her hand on the tabletop— "you don't have to be that anymore." She looked around at the kitchen, at its red walls and the apple-print curtains Margaret had found at a flea market. "You never have to have a white wall anywhere."

The last weight slipped away; the last vestige of her marriage to Brett was gone as surely as if she—with June's help—had swept it out the door. "I do believe," she said, lifting her cup in salute, "this has been the best Thanksgiving I've ever had."

Chapter Thirteen

Ez asked Joss to work with him in the campground office the Monday after Thanksgiving, finalizing things for the partial shutdown. Although the cabins and some of the trailer spaces remained rented, the tent area was closed until spring. The store would remain open, but with limited inventory and hours. Booking and payment could be finalized online, so even the office would be closed much of the time.

She got there before he did and was filing papers when he came in.

He handed her a to-go cup from Romy's. "I know we planned for you to stay in the house until the first of the year, but a party wants to rent it through the holidays, starting the day before Christmas Eve." He wanted to get telling her out of the way first, although her startled look made him wish he'd at least waited until after they'd said good morning. "We don't have to do it. We can stick with the original plan, which I'm fine with, but I wanted to see how you felt about it, especially since I asked you to stay in the house in the first place. You can stay in a cabin, though, if your house isn't ready."

"It's not a problem at all, and it will be great for the campground. The rental house is ready enough."

She looked a little wild-eyed, which was cute on her, but he didn't like having caused it. "It's your fault."

There, that got her. Her eyes calmed and tilted with the beginnings of a smile, and she set down her coffee and planted her hands on her hips. "My fault?"

She had such nice hips…and hands. "Yeah. The pictures of the farmhouse on the campground Facebook page, and that video of us singing in the living room on Thursday seem to have attracted the attention of a family extending from Michigan to southern Georgia looking for a quasi-central location to be together over Christmas."

She knelt in front of the file cabinet again. "I didn't post those pictures."

"I didn't think it was you, but since Gray did, I figured you'd want to take the credit rather than giving it to him. Or the blame, depending on how you look at it."

She frowned momentarily, looking down at the drawer in front of her. "I feel a little sad about leaving Gran's house, but in a way I'm glad to move, because it will be the last time for a while. One of the things I've learned in this long year of discovery is that I don't have vagabond tendencies." She closed the file cabinet with a click of its drawer lock.

He ignored the niggle of gladness that teased his mouth into a smile. "You planning on staying in Banjo Bend?" Surprise and pleasure chased each other across her face.

"I think I am."

"What made you decide that?" *Oh, that's it, McIntire, push her into a corner so she'll feel pressured and un*decide. He shook his head. "Doesn't matter. I'm kind of glad you're staying. If you want to keep

172

working part of the time when the cabins are all finished, maybe we can get the restaurant building ready to lease."

"I'd like that, and I'm hoping Cady needs a part-time person in the library, too. I haven't asked her, but I'm going to. You know, volunteer and try to convince her I'm indispensable."

"You liked working in a library, didn't you?"

She nodded. "It's really the only thing about Dolan Station I miss. Well, a few friends, but not much else."

He would miss her when she moved, even though Dixon Avenue measured out to just one-point-seven miles from his house if you went by way of Colby's Hollow, not much farther than the farmhouse. But she'd become so much a part of the campground, adding color and shine everywhere she went, that he hated the thought of her not being there.

He'd never realized before that he was a fan of color and shine.

"I don't mind at all moving earlier than planned. May I use your truck?" She stood with her hands back on her hips, looking from side to side as if uncertain what to do next. "And for the trips to the thrift stores to get furniture?"

He laughed. "You're looking forward to that part, aren't you?"

"I am. I had so much fun furnishing the farmhouse that I'm looking forward to doing the same thing where I'm going to stay for a while."

Her eyes sparkled with what looked to Ez like anticipation. He didn't understand that, he guessed. When he'd moved down here, Lucy came for a weekend and chose a basic amount of furniture for his house. He liked it fine, and he'd been glad someone else took care of it. Gray told him the interior of the log house looked more like the inside of a nice hotel than someone's home, but he didn't care. It was just a house. A nice one, to be sure, but in the end, no more than a place to sleep.

"Our house in Tennessee was beautiful," she said. "Whatever else I think about Brett, he was a good provider. Working in the library, taking care of our yard—those were things I did because I wanted to, not because we needed for me to. But it wasn't a comfortable place, or friendly. It was tasteful and neutral." She shrugged, opening another drawer and filing the last of the papers. "It was just a house."

That she'd echoed his thought made him smile, although he wasn't sure where she was going with it. "What did you want it to be?"

"I wanted it to be home. I wanted it to feel like the farmhouse does."

"You were in it. That's why the farmhouse feels the way it does. It didn't before you came. It just felt empty—even though there was lots of stuff left there."

She nodded, her lips turned down at the corners. "At first I was 'in' our house. Looking back, though, I'm not so sure I didn't leave it even before I left Brett. It all seems kind of like a dream. At least, after the boys left home. And not such a good dream, either."

He drew down the shades in the office and lowered the temperature on the thermostat. "We all have times like that, I think."

"You, too?"

He nodded, not wanting to pursue the subject.

"If you ever want to talk about them," she said

quietly, pulling on her coat, "I'm a good listener."

****

Allie sent a tiny Christmas tree in a copper pot as a housewarming present. Margaret gave Joss an embroidered tablecloth to cover the deeply scarred top of the round table that Romy had donated from the café for the Dixon Avenue kitchen. Wil DeWitt caned the seats of the four mismatched chairs that surrounded it. Joss painted the chairs sage green.

Two weeks and two days after Thanksgiving, she spent the first night in her new house. She thought, lying in the cozy room under the eaves beneath a quilt Romy made, that with the notable exceptions of the births of Noah and Sam, she'd never been quite this happy. It was the first time in her life her contentment hadn't depended on someone else. Although she'd tried to teach her kids their own happiness was up to them, she hadn't really believed it for herself. She hadn't known how…how to…something. Maybe, like she and Margaret had talked about, she hadn't known how to be Jocelyn Murphy.

She fell asleep right away, but when the phone rang sometime later, she woke disoriented, uncertain of where she was or why she was there. It took a minute, and the phone on the table by the bed had gone silent by the time she picked it up and looked at the missed call. Margaret. Why would Margaret…

Joss frowned and hit the callback button.

"Something's going on at the campground. I heard it on the scanner. A sheriff's car and a firetruck both just went tearing by. Ez doesn't answer his phone."

Joss's heart pounded. "On my way."

"I'll see you there."

It was nice that she slept in sweatpants and a tee shirt, Joss thought abstractedly a few minutes later when she was behind the wheel of her car driving much too fast toward the campground. A peculiar light glimmered over the trees, but she couldn't tell where or what its origin was. Maybe it was just the swirling lights on top of the emergency vehicles. Maybe a campfire had gotten out of control, but that couldn't be. Ez made sure all fires were out before he ended his day. Every day.

What if something had happened to him? What if he'd fallen or if the gun he kept had gone off unexpectedly? Guns did that sometimes. The gun owners she knew swore it never happened, but it only took one time for the wrong hands to get hold of a weapon.

But that couldn't be, either. Ez was even more compulsive about his weapon than he was about everything else. No one else would ever have gotten hold of it unless they disabled him first.

What if he'd—

She couldn't finish the thought. People like Ezra McIntire didn't kill themselves.

People like her didn't get divorced, either, a nasty little voice clamored at the back of her mind, and look how that turned out.

The light grew brighter, and she followed it to the camping trailer-motorhome section of the campground. From somewhere behind her, its wailing siren growing louder by the second, came the ambulance Banjo Bend shared with Colby's Hollow and Wilhelm, a larger town ten miles away. She pulled out of the way and got out of her car, running toward where flames were leaping high and lethal from one of the largest trailers—one that parked here permanently.

Volunteer firefighters worked to contain the fire while campers watched in rapt and horrified silence. Two people, chillingly still, lay on the ground near the sheriff's car well away from the flames, an EMT working urgently over them.

Joss looked, desperate to see who was there, who was hurt. But she couldn't tell.

Where was Ez?

Dear God, where was Ez?

Two other EMTs rushed past her, and she wanted to fall in behind them. Surely she could help, and she'd be able to find out who was hurt. To find out if Ez was one of the people lying too quietly on the ground.

Over the popping and crackling of the fire, she heard the EMTs' repeated requests that people stay back, please stay back. She felt the cold of the night suddenly, even in the burgeoning heat, and feared even more for the ones who were hurt as she pulled her coat closer about her and lifted its hood over her hair.

She stood still, silent and praying. Watching. The fire was abating, being fought by people whose training made them more determined than the licks and cracks of flames that chased them. The EMTs moved fast, economically, and two stretchers wheeled past her faster than she'd have thought possible. She was glad they were hurrying. Surely that meant the victims were alive, didn't it?

One of the EMTs was still there, though, kneeling beside someone who was sitting on a lawn chair that looked ludicrous in the muddy slush. The person had a blanket around him, but—

Joss went toward the man in the chair, circling around another campsite to come up beside him without getting in the way of the emergency personnel. It was cooler here, farther from the waning fire. "Ez." She knelt beside the chair. "Are you all right?"

He looked at her, but she realized instantly he didn't really see her. A chill enveloped her, and she had to stop herself from shaking. His always dark eyes were black, as stark and cold as the obsidian they resembled. She reached to push his hair back from his face and spoke again. "Ez? Will you talk to me?"

"I was too late. Something woke me, and I saw the fire, but it took me too long to get here." He spoke in a monotone that didn't even sound like his voice. "I got them out, but it was too late."

"Sir." The EMT's voice was soothing. "You need to go to the hospital. Your hands are burned, and I don't know how much smoke you inhaled. One of the ambulances will come back as soon as they meet the helicopter."

"Helicopter?" Ez's eyes lit. "I used to fly them. There's nowhere here to set one down here. Where's the helipad?"

"At the clinic in Banjo Bend. It'll only be a little while—"

"No. I don't need to go to the hospital." Ez moved restlessly. "I need to go home and change. I'll have to clean this up as soon as the fire's out, make sure there aren't any embers still burning that can ignite somewhere else."

"Mr. McIntire." It was the sheriff's deputy, kneeling so that he faced Ez. "Do you have a contact number for the owner of the trailer that burned? One of the other campers said you'd probably have it, but none of them did. They said the people you pulled out were the owner's son and a friend. Is that right?"

"Yes," said Joss. Ez still wasn't really tracking, and she bit back fear. "The information is on the office computer. Maybe—" She tried once again to capture Ez's gaze, but he stared past her at the ruins of what had once been a top-of-any-line camping trailer. "Ez, I want to take you to the doctor, okay?" She looked at the EMT. "Will that be okay?"

He nodded, but Ez was shaking his head. "I can't leave," he said. "I can't leave until everyone's taken care of and all right."

"Yes, you can." Margaret's voice reached them as she approached, Wilson following her. She looked at Ez's hands, held out in front of him, and tears flooded her eyes. She brushed them away with an impatient forearm. "Wil and I will make sure everyone gets back to their campsite all right. We'll call Jed to come and help, and we'll all stay here until you and Joss come back from the clinic."

"Can you go to the office with the deputy and find him the phone numbers he needs?" asked Joss.

"Certainly."

"Come on then, Ez. We're going to get those hands prettied up. Can you walk okay?"

He nodded. "I'm fine. But I should stay here."

"We'll come back as soon as you're fixed up, I promise." With the EMT on the other side, she helped him to his feet. He was trembling all over, and she worried for a minute that he would fall and take her down with him, but he steadied himself, and she could feel his strength coming back.

That was encouraging. Medical workers would treat the burns on his hands and ensure that smoke inhalation hadn't done too much harm. A shower would take care of the external damage done by smoke and cinders and drifting ash. He could throw away the clothes he wore. But what would bring him back from whatever corridor of fear or something worse that was holding him prisoner?

She'd learned all she could about PTSD since he'd admitted to suffering from it. Gray had explained still more over Thanksgiving weekend. He'd told her the "little" Ez had mentioned wasn't little at all, but her cousin hadn't given her many details. The story was Ez's to tell, not his.

Driving through the night to the small hospital in Wilhelm after a stop at his house for his phone, wallet, and some bottled water, she wondered if it was a story she'd ever hear. He sat in near silence beside her, his injured hands lying palms-up on his thighs. "Do you want to listen to music?" she asked, when she'd exhausted every avenue of conversation she could think of.

He raised his head suddenly, and she was aware of that stiffening again. And the trembling. Her heart broke a little, and she had to speak past the splintering sensation.

"Ez?"

"Hear them?"

And then she did. The thwapping sound of helicopters overhead. He moved restlessly, and she had an out-of-time memory of being afraid one of the boys would open the car door and fall out while she was driving.

She checked the locks. "They're taking them to Prestonsburg." She wasn't sure if they were or not, but she wanted to calm him…wanted something to loosen the rigidity that had taken over his body. She touched his sleeve lightly, her fingers feeling charred bits of flannel where the fire had evidently licked at the fabric. "Are your arms burned?"

He didn't answer, just stared through the windshield. She supposed he could see the helicopters, although she couldn't.

"I used to fly them."

Repeating himself was so unlike him that it was frightening. "I know. Do you miss it?"

"Not anymore."

As the sound from above dissipated into the darkness, he leaned back.

She thought he closed his eyes.

"Yes."

"You do miss it?"

"No."

He turned his head enough that she could see his frown. He looked petulant, something so out of character it might have made her laugh in a different time and place. A time when pain wasn't a noisy companion in a tension-filled car. "Music. Let's listen to music." He didn't answer, so she went on, forcing briskness into her voice. "Country?"

His tastes were eclectic—they'd had a noisy argument over her dislike for hip-hop. She'd lost—deservedly so, she'd had to admit.

He shrugged, the movement slight. "I don't care. You choose."

She turned on James Taylor, and soon Ez began to

sing along quietly. As she drove, she was conscious of the tension leaving him, easing the atmosphere in the car. Still worried, she laid her hand on his arm, keeping the contact so light it was barely there. There was no distinguishable tremor, no tightening up at her touch. "Feeling better?" She wished she could see his eyes. She was tempted to pull to the side of the road and turn on the overhead lights so that she could, but common sense prevailed.

He nodded. "I wonder if they were cooking meth in there. I should have known that. How could I not have known?"

"How could you have? Did they announce when they drove into the campground what they were going to be doing?"

"They had groceries in the car. It could have been the ingredients."

"The store is closed much of the time. Everyone who camps comes with groceries in the car. If they don't, then there's reason to worry. Not because there are supermarket bags in the backseat."

"Someone has to be responsible."

"I know." She kept her voice soft. "But it doesn't always have to be you, Ez."

The lesson was a hard one for anyone who had an overdeveloped sense of responsibility. Being Cassie's sister had taught her that. Letting recalcitrant teenagers clean up messes of their own making had made her good at it. But it was different for her. She'd come to know Ezra McIntire well enough to realize that.

Trauma room personnel were waiting when Joss pulled up at the hospital. They were helping Ez into a wheelchair by the time she got around the front of the car. "I'll park and wait for you," she promised.

He nodded, not meeting her gaze, and she felt a chill much like the one back at the campground. This must be the disassociation she'd read about that often went with PTSD.

She entered the hospital a few minutes later, told the attendant at the desk where she would be, and went into the deserted waiting room. She felt as if she were losing Ez forever. A voice at the back of her mind reminded her she couldn't lose what she'd never had, but she ignored it. *Having* someone wasn't something to worry about. She'd *had* Brett.

Having connection, though, which she'd come to think she'd had with Ez since the day they'd met in the campground office…that was what she didn't want to lose. She'd never had it with anyone before. Ever. It was both mental and physical, and emotional in a way that went deeper than she could describe.

"Are you family for Ezra McIntire?" A voice came softly from in front of her.

She hadn't even seen anyone come into the waiting room. "No." No one was. That much she did know. "I'm Joss Murphy…a…friend. He doesn't have family here. Can I go in there with him?"

"No, I'm sorry." The woman, wearing a pink vest that identified her as a volunteer, handed her Ez's wallet and phone. "He asked that you hold onto these."

"He didn't ask you to call anyone?"

"No." The woman pointed to a softly lit corner of the room. "There's coffee or tea, if you'd like. I'll come and tell you as soon as there's anything to tell."

Alone again, with a paper cup of coffee on the table beside her, Joss texted Margaret. Because it was only eleven o'clock in Oregon, she called first Sam and then Noah—neither of whom really wanted to talk to his mother late on a Saturday night. As always, though, it was good to hear their voices.

Then there was silence again. She supposed she could have turned on the television that hung on the wall, but the idea held no appeal.

Ez was alone in there. She didn't think he was badly injured, but he wasn't all right, either. The stony dark expression in his eyes stayed with her. Even when he'd talked, it hadn't been communication. He'd been…somewhere else. Some*one* else.

They knew each other's phone passwords, an exchange they'd made one morning when literally no one in the campground office could remember how to get into their phones after an update, so she scrolled through his phone contacts, feeling like a voyeur. She didn't know all that many of the people on his list. Gray, Jed, Lucy—he'd talked about her, but not much—and Joss had never met her. Margaret was next. Seven's name popped up, and she wasn't surprised— she thought he and Gray had invited Ez into their kinship over Thanksgiving weekend.

The list was alphabetical according to first names, just like the one on her phone was. She'd never thought that was reasonable, but she'd gotten used to it. Silas McIntire's name was after Seven's.

Should she? Unless Ez's brother was an extreme night owl, she would wake him if she called, and perhaps alarm him unnecessarily. She didn't even know if Ez would want him to know he'd been hurt, or if Silas was aware of the "little" PTSD his brother suffered.

She thought of Cassie, of her sister's carbon-copy hand in hers on Thanksgiving, and knew without doubt she'd want to know if she was hurt. Before she could change her mind, she tapped on the Missouri number. The groggy voice that answered was as much like Ez's as Cassie's hand was like Joss's.

"Ez?" A split second later, the voice was wide awake. "Something wrong?"

Joss told him who she was and explained what had happened. He listened, asked a few questions that made her aware he knew about the PTSD, and thanked her for calling. He asked her to call back when she knew more. A dog barked in the background.

After hanging up, she walked up and down the hall outside the emergency room, restless and frustrated without anything to do. She remembered historical movies where women had taken to helping mop hospital floors in order to make money or to be available to the loved ones who were there. She wished she had a mop and a bucket.

She couldn't wait to tell Ez that story—she was certain this was the first time in her life she'd ever wanted to mop. They joked a lot about housework because he was actually better at it than she was and minded it a lot less.

"I've never had to clean up after other people," he said. "I imagine you've always done it. From what you've said about living in Dolan Station, it seems as if it was a very traditional neighborhood."

She'd agreed that it was. A few of her friends there hadn't much liked that she did most of the yardwork at the Landry house—they'd worried that it would give their husbands ideas.

Ez had been wrong when he said he'd never had to clean up after other people. She'd come to realize that he did it all the time—both figuratively and literally.

She kept going back to the look in his eyes.

When her cup was empty, she refilled it. She probably didn't need to worry about going back to sleep tonight anyway. She wondered about the two young people Ez had rescued from the burning trailer. She didn't know them, but she knew they were younger than Noah and Sam. They probably had mothers who were journeying through the paths of hell as they worried about their children. Joss prayed…and worried.

Ez was a hero, but at what cost?

She walked more. The small hospital was quiet. Judging by the empty waiting room, Ez must be the only emergency here. It was very different from the Nashville hospitals she had thankfully limited experience with.

"Ms. Murphy?"

Ez's hands were bandaged, and he wore a clean flannel shirt not unlike his own. His face was clean, too. The dark emptiness was gone from his expression, although he didn't yet look like himself, either.

She wished she could think of a better term than "like himself," but she couldn't. She wanted the hint of laughter to come back into his eyes, with that corresponding slight lift to his mouth.

But he could go home.

"He has pain medication onboard," the ER physician said. "We've sent a prescription to the pharmacy that can be picked up in the morning. It will work fine with what he already takes, but he shouldn't be alone tonight. I'd prefer he stay here for observation, but he's pretty adamant that's not going to happen."

"I'll stay with him," Joss promised, "or someone will, anyway."

"He's not deaf." Ez spoke testily from the wheelchair. "You can talk directly to him."

"Except that it wasn't you I was talking to." She was unable to stop herself from grinning in delight that he did indeed *sound* "like himself" even if his eyes were still shadowed. "You ready to go home now?"

"I'm sorry," Ez said quietly, when they were headed back toward the campground. "I'd rather you hadn't seen me like that."

"In pain? I'd rather not have seen that, either."

"That's not what I meant."

"I know." She stopped at an intersection and smiled over at him. "It's not a little PTSD, though, is it?" She wasn't sure talking to him about it was the right thing to do, but she thought ignoring it most certainly was the wrong one.

He didn't answer right away, and she turned the corner. "No," he said quietly, when they'd left the town behind them. "It's pretty big sometimes. It can get real ugly. I take medication, and there's a guy I talk to, but sometimes it still sneaks up behind me. It's like an ambush when it happens. I'm not only unprepared for it, but I'm ticked off about being unprepared."

"Has it ever been mentioned that you should cut yourself some slack?" Her question was a return to the conversation they'd had a few hours before on the way to the hospital, when she'd said he couldn't be responsible for everything. While she laid no claim to expertise, she understood that much.

His chuckle was so quiet it almost wasn't there. "A

time or two."

By the time they got to his house, Margaret had texted that the fire was completely out, and there was nothing more to be done until the next day. A call to the hospital in Prestonsburg connected them to the owner of the destroyed camper. He assured them the two young men Ez pulled from the structure were being kept overnight for observation, but they would be all right. Since Ez had gone in, brought one out, and gone in for the other one, he had probably inhaled more smoke than they had.

"Good." Ez closed his eyes and didn't speak again.

He slept for hours. Joss texted a condition report to his brother, then napped in a chair, but she couldn't relax and ended up working a crossword. In the morning, she checked on him, then went to pick up his prescription. She was tired, but glad to have been able to be where Ez needed her to be. Parking back at his house, she hoped he was still asleep. The ER physician said rest would do more good than the medication.

But he wasn't asleep. He was in his kitchen, coffee in front of him. When she went in, he looked up, his expression so forbidding she almost backed away. She stood still just inside the door, the white bag with the prescription in it still in her hand. "Ez?"

"What were you thinking?" His words fell like splintered ice into the space between them, a space that suddenly seemed huge and impassable. "What were you thinking when you called my brother?"

Chapter Fourteen

Joss laid his prescription on the counter and left through the kitchen door, closing it carefully behind her.

Ez knew she was upset, her pale face and the trembling hand that grasped the doorknob gave that away. A long minute passed before he heard her car drive away. He'd hurt her with his abrupt fury. He knew that—he'd seen the shock on her face when he'd challenged her for calling Silas. He even knew his anger was unreasonable. She had no way of knowing his and his brother's connection wasn't...close. Was hardly even a relationship. That wasn't fair, he recognized—he was the one who distanced himself, not Silas.

Maybe he should go after her and try to explain. He was sure she understood now, after his irate words, that he wasn't a relationship kind of guy and that nothing in his life was to be shared. Nothing of substance, anyway. Even friendships were to float on top of the water, not plunge deep where people could be hurt or drown in angst.

He poured more coffee from the pot she'd made before she went to the pharmacy, his bandaged hands moving awkwardly. He looked at the dark depths of the cup, thinking bourbon might be better, but he'd gotten away from drinking in the morning—even physical pain wouldn't drive him back to it, and he wasn't sure what was in the medication he was on. Besides, Joss's coffee was too good to waste.

He didn't know what he should do. He'd allowed himself to like Jocelyn Murphy too much. To trust her with…with what? More of himself than he should have, he guessed.

She shouldn't have called his brother, although her explanation as to why she had made perfect sense.

Or it would to someone else. Not to him.

"Ez?" Margaret's voice filtered into the kitchen from the front door.

"In here," he called.

She came in, looking as tired as he felt. He gestured toward the coffeemaker and took a seat at the counter.

"How are you feeling?" She got a cup from a cubby.

He almost laughed, because she checked the cup for cleanliness as she always did. Margaret would have hated being referred to as sexist, but she'd never met a man she trusted to clean anything from cups to carpets.

He didn't laugh, although his lips twitched. "All right. Thanks to you and Wil for staying last night. It was mine to do, but…" His voice trailed off. He wasn't seriously going to blame people for being worried about him, was he?

They talked for a while. She showed him pictures on her phone of the site where the fire had been. "We can get it cleaned up as soon as the fire marshal and the sheriff say it's okay. The boy's dad called the office this morning. He's apologetic and will pay all damages."

Dread created a twist in Ez's stomach. "Were they doing meth?"

Margaret shook her head. "I don't know, and I don't think he does, either, but he knows his boy and his friend were responsible."

That was a relief. Ez had good insurance, but the worry about minors doing drugs or consuming liquor at the campground was a weight on his shoulders. Was he going to have to get dogs to sniff out illegal activity? The thought was depressing, although it made him think of Elwood and Jake—they'd have been good at something like that.

Margaret got up, rinsing her cup and putting it away. She got the coffee maker ready to turn on, then wiped the granite counter and island the way he'd seen every woman he knew do even when the surfaces were clean. She turned to look at him. "Are you hungry?"

"No." His stomach told him he should eat, but he thought it might turn on him if he tried. Joss had left him some coffee cake when she went to the pharmacy, but Silas called before he got a chance to eat it.

The conversation with his brother went all right, really. Stilted, the way it often was, but he'd sensed Silas's concern. He even offered to fly to Kentucky to help him out for a few days, but Ez knew he didn't mean it. "I can come," Silas said, but Ez demurred. Too much water had flowed under the bridge for that. What was he thinking? There was no bridge.

He wished he'd closed the campground down completely for the winter. If he had, there'd be time to clear the mess left by the fire and make needed improvements throughout the property. If he had closed down, the fire would never have happened. Two college kids might not be in a hospital.

He was surprised when Joss said they were being released today. He'd been so sure he was too late. Again.

"Ezra?"

He looked up at where Margaret stood, hands on her hips, her forehead creased with concern or irritation—he wasn't sure which. He wondered how many times she'd said his name without him hearing her. Often enough for her to resort to calling him "Ezra." That's how his mother used to get his attention, too.

"What?"

"Are you all right? Do you want me to stay with you, or is Joss coming back over?"

Probably not. He didn't say the words, though, just shook his head. "I'm fine here. I'm doped up enough I'm just going to give myself the day off. I have food and stuff to drink. Thanks, Margaret."

"Keep your phone with you."

"I will." As soon as he found it, anyway. He didn't remember where he'd left it after talking to Silas.

He finished his coffee, ate a piece of cake, and fell back to sleep in front of the television, waking sluggish and unaccountably lonely shortly after noon. His hands hurt, and he'd been taking medication long enough to understand the origin of his lethargy. But loneliness wasn't something he would make room for. Life was enough of a challenge without that.

Hunger made itself felt, and he went into the kitchen. A note was on the island. Joss's neat script instructed him on where she'd left food for his lunch and how to heat it up. An orange dinner plate sat on a turquoise placemat beside the note. A paper plate with a dozen cookies was neatly wrapped in plastic. A book, the one she'd promised to give him when she finished it, lay next to them. His coffee cup was there, too. So was his bourbon glass.

He was better alone, he assured himself, warming the roast and potatoes and uncovering the dish of green beans she'd left. No one got hurt when he was on his own. No one needed space he was loath to give up. He smiled grimly, sitting at the island and opening the book. No one minded that he read at the table, either.

Not only was he better alone, he *liked* it. The real reason he never stayed in a relationship was easily explained—he just didn't play well with others. But for the first time, his own company wasn't enough, or even in the ballpark of enough. The loneliness he'd woken with was like a headache that wouldn't go away. His phone was unusually silent. Jed was at the office and would stay there until all the campers had checked out. He'd field any campground calls.

The temperature had gone up this morning, although the sun stayed hidden, making it a muddy, dreary, sluggish kind of day. He put on a jacket, easing the sleeves over his hands, and took his coffee to the porch. Even the creek looked moody. And lonely.

****

Stay busy. Joss learned that when Noah and Sam started school. She did what her friends did, volunteered here and there, joined two book clubs, and went to the gym to battle the extra fifteen pounds that had accompanied her much of her adult life. She was a room mother a few times, until the boys asked her not to do it anymore—at which point she baked cookies

193

and facilitated fundraisers.

When the twins were in middle school, the library where she spent much of her volunteer time offered her a job. Brett hadn't liked it that she suddenly had to consider a schedule other than the one marked on the whiteboard calendar in the kitchen. But she'd loved busyness. She still did.

This day, when she'd been startled by the fury in Ez's voice and angry with herself because she'd once again obviously read more into their relationship than was there, she needed to be busy. Rearranging comfort into her little house lent vicarious consolation, too.

When she took his lunch to his house, she'd intended to stay and try to talk it out with him, but in the end thought better of it. He'd been mad, and after she'd explained her reasoning for calling his brother, he'd still been mad. It was up to him now. She spent half her married life walking on tiptoe so she wouldn't offend Brett for one reason or another—that wasn't a habit she planned to take up again.

Admitting—not for the first time—that it had *been* a habit at all took some of the indignant wind out of her sails. Of all the things she'd never wanted to be, a doormat was somewhere near the top of her list. And yet she was having to admit the reality of it again and again.

She walked to the library to return books and pick up a few more. After talking to Cady for a while and running a duster over the tops of some of the bookcases, she smiled at the young librarian. "Do you get bored?" she asked. "There isn't much to do here. I probably wouldn't have liked that when I was your age."

"I do sometimes," Cady admitted, "and I'm dreading winter a little bit. I like it here, really I do. But I was looking for something when I came, and I'm not sure it's here. Does that make sense?"

"Perfect sense." Joss's response was heartfelt. "Do you know what you were looking for?" She brought the duster over and put it away in the cupboard behind the desk that held day-to-day cleaning supplies.

"Roots. Being from a career military family makes it difficult to establish them. But we were here for vacation when Dad was stationed at Fort Knox, and I loved it."

"I love it here, too."

"I appreciate your help." Cady's gaze met hers, and her smile faded. "Are you all right? You're pale."

"Just tired."

She stopped at Romy's and ordered a meal for Ez. "Will you take it to him when you get off?" she asked. "I really don't feel very well tonight."

It was true. She was tired, and she thought having a heartache qualified her for not feeling well. She walked to the little house on Dixon Avenue and let herself in, looking around at its pretty colors, brightened still more by Christmas decorations. Had it been just last night that she'd lain in bed under the eaves and thought about how happy she was?

The boys' phone numbers tempted her. They were the only part of her life that remained intact. She could call just to hear their voices, to laugh at Noah's winery stories and Sam's excitement about the kids on his basketball team. If she talked to them, she could feel like herself again.

She'd been so sure only hours before that this was

where she wanted to stay. She knew who she was here. At least, she thought she had, before the man she was almost certainly falling in love with had turned on her. With a glass of wine and a plate of cheese and crackers in front of her, she sat at the little table with a crossword, a hard one that would demand all of her mind.

One particular word required a full glass of white zinfandel, three crackers, and three pieces of cheese. She'd seen if before, although she'd never used it in conversation. *Truculent.* Uncertain of its exact meaning, she looked it up. "Aggressively self-assertive, belligerent; scathingly harsh, vitriolic…" suggested *Merriam-Webster*.

Ezra McIntire.

The thought made her laugh, although the wine might have had a little to do with it, too. One day of truculence wasn't going to scare her. Not now. Not in Act Two.

****

Ez probably could have driven into Banjo Bend the next day, but his hands still hurt, so he went on foot. He took the back way through Colby's Hollow, thinking he'd walked more since coming to Banjo Creek than he had since basic training. He'd always ridden his bicycle on campus—many of the faculty had.

The temperature was unseasonably warm, and the wind had lain down to where it was only a minor rustle in the trees. He was glad to be outside.

He needed to see Joss.

By the time he reached the brick house on Dixon Avenue, he was tired. And glad to see her car in her driveway. He wasn't ready for the walk back to his house. He didn't know if she'd talk to him after his behavior the day before, but he hoped she at least wouldn't send him packing before he'd had a chance to get some rest.

She didn't smile when she opened the door. She didn't hurry him inside or apologize for something that hadn't been her fault to begin with or look with overdone concern at his bandaged hands. She stood quietly, waiting for him to make the first move.

Which he thought he'd already made. Coming here after he'd been rude and accusatory the day before had taken more courage than he'd expected. Admitting that, even to himself, made his mouth lift in a half smile. He'd faced gunfire more than once, for heaven's sake, yet he was afraid of a small woman with red hair and a sprinkling of freckles across her nose? "I'm sorry." There, that wasn't so bad. "I was wrong." That was a little harder. "I have no excuse." That should stop the discussion he knew she'd want to have. That he *didn't* want to have.

"I'm not interested in excuses anyway." Her voice was cool but not unfriendly.

At least, he hoped it wasn't.

"Reasons, on the other hand—I might be interested in those."

"You probably wouldn't."

"I spent twenty-five years with a man who thought he never had to explain himself. I was there by choice, and no one forced me to stay, but it's not a situation I'll entertain again. We can either be honest with each other, or we can call it a day."

Her voice started out crisp but trembled at the end, and he realized standing up for herself came no more easily to her than explaining himself did to him. As Margaret would say, with a wry twist to her mouth, *what a novel concept.* "May I come in?"

She stepped back, and he went into the house, stopping just inside the door and putting his arms around her. It was awkward, with his oven-mitt-type hands, but she didn't pull away, just slipped her arms around his waist and leaned in.

"Si was always the good son. He never meant to be, and the old man didn't like him any better than he did me, but he still used us against each other, and we let him do it until there was no bridging the divide." He spoke over the top of her head, forcing the words out and knowing they weren't reason enough for him to have turned on her.

She leaned back, her hands on his chest, her gaze arrowing sharply in on his. "Why don't you fix it?"

"Because it's been too long. We're not going to come together the way your family did at Thanksgiving. We are just him and his kids and me, and we're a wallet family—we send each other pictures. I send money for graduations and weddings. Silas sent a case of wine when I bought the campground. I don't go back to the farm to visit. He doesn't come here."

The loneliness hit again, sharp and aching regardless of the woman he held in his arms. He thought of Gray and, as glad as he always was to talk to and see his friend, he still missed his brother.

"I'll bet he would." She drew away and led the way to her little round table.

I can come. Silas's words echoed in his mind. "Maybe." He shrugged off his jacket and sat where she indicated he should.

She brought coffee to the table and more of the coffee cake from the day before. "It's nice seeing the people who share your history," she said, "not just because you've told it to them but because they were there with you when it happened."

Gray had understood the PTSD when it struck and when it struck again because he'd been there the first time. But Silas understood the roots of it in ways no one else ever could.

I can come.

That explained the loneliness. As simple as the explanation was, it made Ez feel better. Well, that and being in Joss Murphy's kitchen, drinking her coffee, and being nearly certain she'd forgiven him for being a total jerk.

She held her cup between her hands. "I may have overstepped when I called your brother." Her voice was soft but her gaze across the table direct. "The truth is that I would do the same thing again. I also over-reacted to your anger." She shrugged. "I'll probably do that again, too. I don't like confrontation."

"It's okay." He took her hand and held it against his cheek, feeling the heat from the cup and the additional warmth that was just hers. "We're okay. Right?"

She nodded, her smile lighting the room. "What are your plans for the day?"

"I don't have any," he admitted. "I always work, and even if I don't, I play guitar. I can't do either of those things, so the day's just out there. Empty."

She eyed him thoughtfully, and he noticed for the first time that she looked extraordinarily tired, her natural paleness accentuated by dark circles under her eyes.

That was his fault. For a moment, he considered apologizing again, but there wasn't substance in apology without change. "Maybe—" he began, and then stopped. *Maybe what?*

The centerpiece on the table, a group of flickering snowman candles surrounded by greenery and a plaid ribbon, caught his attention. "Maybe a Christmas tree. I've never bothered with one, but I've never owned a house before, either. Would you like to take me to get one? I have decorations and lights in a box, because people always give them to me in the hope that Scrooge will give in one year. Maybe this is the year."

"I'd like that. A real one or artificial?"

"A real one." If he hated having a tree, he could haul the real one out of the house the day after Christmas, burn it, and never have to have another. Artificial ones tended to stay. They took up spaces in closets and attics and created bursts of memories every time a person tripped over the box. He had enough things tripping him up, including the box of ornaments that had been all over the world with him.

"Let's go get your truck."

Joss's suggestion brought him back to the present. Twenty minutes later, they were on their way to the Christmas tree farm halfway between Banjo Bend and Wilhelm.

"Did you have real trees when you were a kid?" she asked.

"We did when Mom was alive. When she was gone, we didn't do Christmas anymore. The old man couldn't stand it." He hesitated, a long-buried memory forcing itself out. "She died during the holidays. Si and

I were playing basketball, and Dad went to the game. When we got home, she was gone. She'd had a heart attack and died instantly. He never forgave either himself or us for not being there when she needed us."

Joss braked, smoothly but suddenly, and came to a stop at the side of the road, looking at him across the console of the truck. "Is that how long you've felt responsible for the whole world, Ez? Since your mother died?"

Chapter Fifteen

Ez would have been perfectly content with a Charlie Brown tree he could set on top of a table and forget about until he could safely get rid of it, but Joss hadn't been buying and putting up Christmas trees her entire adult life for nothing. She knew there was a reason the person who designed his house did it with ten-foot ceilings and a wall of windows and doors in the living room facing the creek.

That reason was almost certainly because it provided a perfect spot for a nine-foot-and-change Fraser fir.

"Are you serious?" Ez looked up at the tree she'd chosen. "It's twice your size and I'm"—he held up his hands—"incapacitated."

"Jed will help," she said, hoping she was right. "So will Wyatt. All you'll have to do is supervise." She grinned and added a flirtatious wink. It felt ridiculous, but fun, too. "You're good at that."

While the tree was loaded into the truck, Joss bought a pair of wreaths to hang on the front and back doors of her house. When she got behind the wheel, Ez gave her a look so put-upon she almost laughed out loud.

His sigh nearly shook the truck. "Okay, now that I have a tree that would be right at home in Rockefeller Center, I'd like to take you to lunch, but would you mind going to a drive-through? These hands make eating in front of anyone an extreme social blunder."

"I'll fix sandwiches. That be all right?" She knew the contents of his refrigerator well enough to know what they could have.

"Yes." He smiled, although it wasn't a happy expression. "Thanks, Joss."

"You're welcome."

A truck sat in his driveway when they got to his house, one that was exactly like his, only red instead of black.

"Expecting someone?" She pulled up beside the other vehicle. Someone was sitting in one of the rockers on the back porch, though, holding a bundle in his lap.

"I'll be damned."

Ez had the door open and was out of the truck before she even had the engine turned off. Once he was out, though, and halfway to the porch, his step slowed and she was able to catch up with him. She put her hand on his sleeve, worried about the tension that radiated from him.

"Ez." The man on the porch got to his feet.

Joss felt her mouth drop open. Although she knew Ez and Silas weren't twins, they looked nearly as much alike as Sam and Noah did. Silas was an inch or so taller and not quite as broad, but when he stepped off the porch, his gait matched his brother's. He was clean shaven, and his hair more neatly cut, but his eyes were the same. His smile was the same, too, although Joss would have been willing to bet his came easier and more often.

He was carrying something black and white.

"She's a girl," he said without preamble, "but she's

a granddaughter of Elwood a couple of generations back, so I named her Ellie. I think you'll like her." Without ceremony, he put the puppy into Ez's arms and offered his hand to Joss. "You must be Joss. I'm Silas. Thank you for calling me. He never would have."

His hand even felt like Ez's. Strong and hardworking, with well-kept nails. "I'm happy to meet you. You're just in time to help get this behemoth into the house." She gestured toward the tree in the bed of Ezra's pickup.

The three of them manhandled the tree inside and got it standing semi-straight in the blessedly heavy-duty tree stand they'd bought at the tree farm. Joss made fresh coffee and sandwiches while the brothers argued over which side was the best one. She took little Ellie outside so she could use the facilities and went back in. "I'm going home now," she announced even though neither of the men was paying the slightest bit of attention. "Ellie probably likes me better than either of you and would like to go with me, but I've told her she can visit often."

Ez blinked. "Leaving? Why don't you stay? We were going to have lunch."

She grinned at them both. "Lunch is in the kitchen whenever you're ready to eat it, but I'm going home. I'm the mother of brothers. I've seen what they look like when they're together after time apart, although Sam and Noah have seldom *been* apart. It all gets down to using words I never allowed in the house, drinking more than they should, and possibly smoking things I also didn't allow in the house. They don't need me around then, and neither do you."

Ez kissed her goodbye, right in front of Silas,

which she enjoyed. She waved at them both, reassured Ellie that she would see her later, and left the house on the creek. She walked home the long way, taking time to check the cleanup in the camper section of the campground and ensuring the office and the restaurant buildings were locked. Sometimes people got curious and didn't mind jimmying locks to satisfy that curiosity.

She slowed her pace as she passed the farmhouse. "You'd like it, Gran," she murmured aloud, standing in front of it. "And you'd love the color it's going to be."

The house would be red in the spring, with new charcoal shutters and cream-colored trim. The barn behind the house, red for as long as Joss remembered, would be painted the dark gray of the shutters, while its window trim and the crossbars on the doors would echo the cream on the house.

Standing at the gate, Joss knew she would be here to see it. She continued the walk toward the little house on Dixon, remembering a few nights before, when she'd settled into the bed under the eaves and reveled in the feeling of happiness.

She celebrated again.

****

"What made you come?" Ez didn't know why he asked the question—its answer didn't matter. He was gladder to see his brother than he ever in a million years would have anticipated.

"Ellie peed on the kitchen rug. It was either shoot the dog or bring her to you."

Ez snorted. "You'd shoot me before you'd shoot a dog."

"Only if you peed on the rug."

Ellie snuggled in beside Ez in his chair, laying her chin on his leg and staring blissfully at him. When he looked at her and petted her with the parts of his hands that weren't bandaged, he felt perilously close to tears.

The thought horrified him. That wasn't happening. He didn't care how glad he was to see his brother or the puppy who might or might not be allowed to sleep on his bed.

He'd need to put a chair beside the mattress so she wouldn't fall off.

"I talked to my kids after Joss called me," said Silas. He leaned back in the other recliner. "They're all fine. Your niece offered to come and stay with you. However, she is pregnant and hormonally awful. My son-in-law, Brady, might have to live with her, but you don't. Actually," he added, grinning, "Brady offered to leave Mary with me and come take care of you himself. Patrick wishes you well. John Ezra wanted to come with me, but he's in Park City for the winter."

Ez thought of his niece and nephews. Pretty Mary married right out of high school against everyone's advice and had spent the last six years making a success of her life's choice. Davis, the eldest, farmed the land Silas and Ez grew up on and still owned. John Ezra was the family adventurer. At twenty-two, he was a ski valet in Utah during the winter, worked at an apple orchard in Indiana in autumn, and was a personal watercraft guide in Key West during the summer.

They were such great kids, more attentive to their grumpy uncle than he was to them. "Thank them for me." Maybe, if he asked, they'd come to visit.

"Do it yourself," Silas suggested. "You got any beer?"

"In the fridge."

"You want one?"

He started to refuse, but he remembered that the doctor had said one or two beers or glasses of wine would be okay. "Yeah. I'd like that."

Silas went into the kitchen, coming back with two cans and two glasses, including Ez's favorite one. "It's okay for you to have this?"

Ez nodded. "No bourbon, though. This might be a good time to stop that anyway. I think—" He stopped, not sure what he wanted to say, then forged ahead. "I probably come way too close to abusing it." He knew he wasn't an alcoholic. He'd spent enough time with counselors and psychologists to be certain of that, but he'd purposefully overlooked signs of alcohol abuse sometimes.

Less lately. Since the day Joss Murphy drove into the campground.

"Davis wants to open a winery on the farm. You know, like we always wanted to? I don't want to discourage him the way the old man always did us, but I worry about him losing everything. Not the farm—it's ours—but all of his own money." Silas shrugged. "I'm not going to try to stop him, though. He's an adult."

But won't you feel responsible? If you could have stopped him from making the mistake of his life and you let him do it, won't you feel as if it was your fault? Ez had to stop the words from bursting forth. The problem was with him, not his brother, and yet… "Don't you…" His voice faded.

"My job is to be his wingman. I'll do what I can to help him without interfering, but in the end, he's the one piloting the plane. Or helicopter, to keep it in truly familial terms." Silas held his gaze. "Your job, Uncle Ez, is to be a secondary wingman. But if he fails, it's not because of anything you or I did or didn't do." He leaned toward Ez, his eyes still intent, his voice firm. "He's the pilot," he repeated.

I was the pilot, too.

But the words he'd said to himself all this time didn't hold the power they used to. What had happened after he set the chopper down hadn't been anything he could control. He couldn't have known his former student was going to enter his classroom with murder on his mind, either. Both events had been awful, terrible things, but not ones he could have changed if he'd done something right.

Because the truth was, he hadn't done anything wrong.

He couldn't have stopped the fire in the campground. He was sorry the kids had gotten hurt, but it could have been much worse than it had been. Just as he had in Iraq and in his classroom, he'd reacted as fast and as well as he could.

He hadn't done anything wrong.

The conversation with Joss on the way to the Christmas tree farm, recent enough he could still hear its words, came back to him. *Is that how long you've felt responsible for the whole world, Ez? Since your mother died?*

He'd denied it, although without any heat, and changed the subject as quickly as he could. Yet here it was again, and this time there could be no denial. This time Silas, who'd surely blamed himself as much as Ez had, was the one waiting to hear what he had to say. "We couldn't have saved Mom."

"No." Silas shook his head. "But I'm sure we've both tried to figure out how we could have a thousand times over the years. Something I've learned from being a dad is that the old man had some things to answer for. Letting us think it was our fault Mom died is one of them."

For the first time, Ez understood his brother's anger. "I stuck you with him, didn't I? I know I sent money and that I made an annual duty visit so you could get away, but I never stayed. I wouldn't have, so you had to. I'm sorry."

Silas shook his head. "I was the oldest, and I was the one who wanted to farm. It stood to reason I'd be the one to stay. I can look back and see where I made you think I blamed you for leaving. I never did. I was probably mad at myself for staying. A few remarks from Jackie about 'choosing the wrong brother' didn't help matters, either."

Ez had wondered if his name had ever come up. He'd liked Jackie, but that had been all. "I never—"

"I know. I always knew. It wasn't you." Silas's lips lifted into a smile that was like looking in the mirror. "Make no mistake, though—I *wanted* it to be you. Realizing several years into the marriage that I was second choice wasn't a happy thing." He took a long drink of his beer. "She told me, after we were divorced, that she'd called you."

"I was embarrassed for her," Ez admitted, "and I didn't want you to know she'd called, in case you worked things out."

His brother nodded, and the weight shifted.

"I'm glad Joss called you," Ez's voice was roughened by emotion. He smiled down at Ellie, who sat up and took notice of the expression. "And thank you for bringing her. I really wanted a dog."

"I'm glad, too." Silas cleared his throat. "But you need to realize she doesn't know she's a dog. I've never told her."

"Oh." Ez covered the puppy's silky ears. "She won't hear it from me."

Chapter Sixteen

"They what?" Joss set down her fork and stared across the table at Ez, who didn't even look upset. He was exchanging looks of mutual admiration with Ellie.

"The kid's dad's lawyer said he should sue the campground, that we should have been aware they were cooking meth in the camper."

"That's just craziness. He should—"

"The kid's dad said he thought maybe he should get a new lawyer. As soon as we're released to clean up from the fire, he's bringing a crew that includes his son and his son's friend. I think he has every intention of working their entitled young tails off."

She laughed, remembering the Saturday Noah and Sam had spent repainting the restrooms at the clubhouse in Dolan Station. They hadn't been the only ones who vandalized them, but she'd been the only parent who made them do reparation. "Are you going to let them?"

"I am." He got up, taking their dishes to the sink. He still moved his hands gingerly, but six days after the fire, the bandages were off. "Ellie needs a walk, and I need to talk to you. Want to do the rounds with me?"

"Sure." She looked at Silas. "Are you coming, too?"

"No. Ez said since you cooked and he supervised, I had to stay here and load the dishwasher. Go figure.

Ellie's going, though." Silas pointed at the puppy where she sat patiently near the door with her leash in her mouth.

The night was clear and cold, lit by a starry sky and the Christmas lights that were everywhere in the sparsely populated campground. Joss tucked her arm through Ez's as they walked, feeling the warmth where he held her hand against his side. Ellie, her leash unused in the pocket of Ez's coat, trotted ahead, as if to show her humans the way.

"I think I told you I've been on sabbatical from the college," he said. "Not that I ever thought I'd go back, but it was a bridge I managed not to burn on my way out the door anyway."

She nodded, wondering where the conversation was going. She thought he was a born teacher—she'd watched him with different groups at the campground. All the way from guitar players who'd sat in a circle and watched his fingers to the fifth graders he accompanied on their leaf collection hunts, his "students" had listened and absorbed. In the office, when he instructed employees in how he wanted things done, they almost all got it the first time. Even Margaret, who made a great pretense of ignoring him, did as he asked because his explanation always made sense.

He stepped onto the porch and checked the door on the restaurant building, then rejoined her on the path. "But they asked me."

They walked in silence for a few beats. "Asked you?"

"To come back. To teach a few classes and help with the creation of a few more. They've…the students have been successful. The college thinks…and I think…I have more to offer them." He met her eyes. "I want to do it."

"It sounds exciting." More to the point, *he* sounded excited. His voice held a ripple she hadn't heard before. But he also sounded…scared. "Ez?"

He was silent, but his arm was tight against his side, keeping her hand there so that she couldn't have pulled it away if she wanted to. Even when they reached the first cabin, he kept hold as he went onto the porch and checked the locks. Ellie waited for them to go on, finally lying down on the path if they tarried too long.

Not until they reached the pavilion did Ez say more than one desultory, "The Christmas lights on the porches look good, don't they?" The rest of the time, all Joss could hear was their footsteps and Ellie's eager panting.

They passed the fireplace at one end of the structure, checking on the wood supply and stepping over to where they could look out over the creek, dark and star-spangled.

"It was just another day," he said.

His voice was quiet enough Joss had to strain to hear. She waited, understanding the phrase about your heart being in your throat—she thought hers was lodged there.

"Isn't that how all horror stories start? Class was almost done…like within five minutes. The door burst open, and there he was, wild-eyed and seeming to be bristling with guns, just the way a shooter would be in the movies. He'd been in that class the year before, and he was smart, but I gave him a failing grade anyway.

There was no way around the flunk—he didn't show up to class half the time, and he didn't do the work *any* of the time."

Unable to stop the reaction, Joss gasped. "How did he get there without being stopped?"

"He broke in the night before and left his weapons in the closet of an unused classroom. He was very familiar with the building." Ez shook his head. "I say he was 'bristling with guns,' but in actuality, he had two. They were meant for the business at hand, though. He'd sprayed the room with bullets before another student and I were able to subdue him. Other than cuts from glass flying everywhere, no one was seriously hurt. I have no idea to this day how that happened, other than there'd been enough school shootings that the students knew how to react."

"That's when you came here?"

"No." He shook his head. "That came at midterms when I had to flunk a kid, just the way I'd flunked the shooter the year before. All of a sudden I couldn't walk back into the classroom. Lucy even had to go in and get my personal stuff so an adjunct could use the room. I called Gray, and pretty soon I was here."

Heaviness settled in around her heart. She knew then why he'd wanted to talk. He was better. Not just his hands, but his state of mind. She could tell that even in the week since the fire. Silas's coming had given Ez some puzzle answers he'd never been able to solve on his own.

The campground was a safe place, a haven for healing not just for Ez but for visitors and employees, too. Only he didn't need it anymore. "You've come a long way." She hoped her voice didn't sound as hollow as she felt.

"I think I have, too. A long enough way that I want to go back," he said again. "I'm not positive I can, but I think so." He knelt, his back to her, and stroked Ellie's silky head lightly and gently. "I know so."

Joss thought so, too, and she was happy for him. Really, she was. She wanted him to find the peace inside himself she'd found under the eaves in the little house on Dixon.

But the truth was that she'd wanted him to find it here.

With her.

For the second time in her life, Jocelyn Murphy was in love, and it was so different than she'd ever had any idea it could be. In the earliest days of her marriage, she'd felt completed by her love for Brett, although it didn't always make her happy. Now, she was complete on her own. She wasn't yet sure she wanted to share an address or even a toothpaste tube with Ezra McIntire, but loving him *did* make her happy.

She'd lived long enough to know that finding happiness at the cost of someone else's wasn't a winning proposition. At least, not for her. "You should go." She kept her breathing even, with no small effort.

He raised his eyes then, meeting her gaze with a pleased smile. "I think so, too."

She thought, for just a minute, of buying the campground. If she cashed in her retirement savings and went back to work fulltime somewhere that offered health insurance, she could probably pull it off. For that matter, Brett might help her obtain financing— after all, it was what he did for a living. Maybe some of the cousins would be interested in buying in, too.

Would she still feel the same about the property if Ez wasn't part of the package? That wasn't something she could answer.

They left the pavilion, walking toward the camper area, lit not only by security lighting but by decorated trailers and motor homes.

"Will you sell the campground right away?" She forced the words out. "Or will you wait a while to be sure it works out at the college?"

He stopped so suddenly that Ellie went on without them for a few feet and turned back to look, aggrieved at being deserted.

Ez knelt to comfort the pup, looking up at Joss. "What do you mean?"

"If you move back to Virginia, won't you sell the campground?"

"No." His answer was immediate and adamant. "I'll get an apartment off-campus. I'll only be there a few days a week."

"Oh." The relief made her feel a little lightheaded...not to mention goofy. She'd gone from being a self-reliant single woman to being an adolescent-with-a-crush in less than a thousand feet.

He straightened, leaving Ellie in a paroxysm of wiggling extasy. "Wil and Margaret can run the place better than I do, especially if Jed stays around. I think there's something my nephew and your son who's a winemaker would be interested in, too. Silas and I are talking about buying the old winery over at Colby's Hollow—it's across the county line."

"But the college is four hours away." She was bewildered by how casual he was being about what seemed to her an impossible commute. And yet, against her better judgment, hope unfurled like a spring flower. "How will you do everything?"

He laughed, putting his arm around her and tugging her in close. "How did you do everything when you worked a job and raised kids and kept a house? I'm more than one thing, Joss, just as you are and everyone is. I was convinced that being a loser who let people die and get hurt on his watch was all I was. But I was wrong."

She understood then. She'd come to Banjo Bend feeling like nothing more than an ex-wife, a no-longer-needed mother, and an easily laid-off library employee. Who she'd become since stopping at Romy's Café that first time was much more. Over and above that, she liked the woman in her mirror these days.

"It's like the puzzles." He stood still, turning her to him and lifting her face with a finger under her chin. "You know, the hard ones we do. They are so complicated, but satisfying, too. They're all jagged on the page, with the little squares going in here and out there depending on the length of the words. Yet they come together, and the words all fit."

Oh, that was perfect. "I'm glad you're not leaving. I'd like…" She stopped. She wasn't a girl who'd ever called and asked a guy for a date. She hadn't told Brett she loved him until he said it first. She would never— Or would she?

"I like you so much," she said in a rush, holding his gaze. "It was scary, feeling that…much for someone. And unexpected, you know? I probably will make mistakes, because it's all new to me, but I'd like to be close, to have a…a relationship. A real one. But only if that's what you want, too."

She thought she might have aged ten years in one paragraph. She could stand up for herself when she needed to. She could refuse to do things like paint walls white, read a bestseller simply because it was popular, or have her eyes "done" because her mother said she was showing her age. Laying her feelings out there to get trampled was something altogether different.

What if he didn't answer? Or if he did answer, but she didn't want to hear what he had to say? Or— But then she was in his arms, being held so close it was hard to breathe. But breathing was overrated sometimes, wasn't it?

"I want that, too." His voice was rough, and his heart beat hard and fast against her ear. "I don't have the right words, and the pieces of me are as jagged as the puzzle, but I'd love to finish it together. You don't have to fix me—" He drew back enough that they could look into each other's eyes again, but he didn't let her go. "I'm not going to fix you, either, if some of your clues aren't working, but I'll help you with them."

"I'll help you, too." She was so filled with glee she'd love to have a Mary Tyler Moore moment and throw her hat into the air, but she knew herself well enough to realize the hat would get stuck in a tree, and Margaret had made it for her. She didn't want anything to happen to it.

"In that case, you need to pay attention to this, because my knees are too creaky to do it again." With Ellie dancing delighted attendance, Ez knelt on one knee, holding Joss's hands in his. "It can be a relationship if that's what you want," he said, his gaze warm and steady on hers, "but would you give some thought to marrying me instead? It can be as soon or as long from now as you say. Going slow can be good…I know that, but sometimes it's also like having white walls—life's too short for it."

"Well, then." She smiled, although she felt tears tangling in her lashes at the same time. "We don't want to wait around, do we?"

Epilogue

They planned to marry in spring, when the greens of season's changing were fresh and bright. The semester at the college would be done, and Ez would be back in Banjo Bend full-time, teaching a few summer classes remotely. They could decide whether they would live in his house on the creek or convert it to a rental and live on Dixon Avenue. There was plenty of time, after all.

But then Noah and Sam showed up unexpectedly three days before Christmas. Noah picked up the cases of wine he'd shipped ahead. Sam complained they left no room in the rental car for luggage.

Their mother was beside herself with joy.

Anxious to see each other again because the Thanksgiving gathering had been so much fun, the Murphy cousins, aunts, and uncles arrived over the next twenty-four hours. Marley, looking better than she had three weeks before, was thrilled to see everyone she'd just seen "yesterday." She painted a picture of Joss and "the big boy who's Ellie's dad" standing in the pavilion looking out at a rainbow over Banjo Creek.

Silas mentioned going home, but instead he called his kids and invited them to come to Banjo Bend to spend Christmas. They agreed happily.

All of the cabins ended up being occupied. When asked, the owners of a few of the RVs that stayed in the